Autobiography

from

Dea APHRODITE-KALI

"Who is Dea APHRODITE-KALI?"

or

"I Fioretti di san Francesco d'Assisi"

Autobiography

from

Dea APHRODITE-KALI

Production and publishing house:
Books on Demand GmbH, Norderstedt, Germany
ISBN 9783842375260

Imprint

The German national-library records this publication in the German national-bibliography; elaborate bibliographical data are accessible in the Internet under http://dnb.d-nb.de

Editor:

Evelyn TURIANO
Postfach 200355
D-13513 Berlin
Germany

© 2010, 2011 Copyright by Evelyn TURIANO & Dea APHRODITE-KALI
Berlin - Germany
All right reservations.

Authoress and translator to English language:

Dea APHRODITE-KALI
Postfach 200355
D-13513 Berlin
Germany

{The authoress and editor refers on theirs right at the "articles 5 that German Constitution"!}

1. Edition August 2011

Production and publishing house:

Books on Demand GmbH, Norderstedt, Germany

ISBN 9783842375260

Content

<u>Preliminary note</u>

In the fifties year, many Catholic hospitals did experiments with embryos and babies in Europe.
"Dea APHRODITE-KALI, born Froletti" is a matter of one "failed fruit" from one of these experiments.

Although the authoress has written the history of Dea APHRODITE-KALI with a mixture of modern fable, thriller, intrigues, love affair, sexual-misuses, documentary-reports and so on, is about a true history.
The authoress had summarized all memories, also about nightmares, medical and judicial reports about Dea APHRODITE-KALI just like a puzzle-picture.
Dea APHRODITE-KALI, a so-called daughter of the Vatican, was born in a special-department of a Milanese hospital, where in the fifties year and probably certainly still nowadays, on order and supervision of the Vatican under questionable experiments, nuns have born babies.
Of course, the reader stands freely to believe this history or not.
He/she can does also own investigations, that deny this history or confirm.

The prehistory (1950-1951)

It was in the year 1950 once, as Agnese Vittoria Fioraso a 24-year old young woman, her home-village of Sarego/Italy leaves and is to Milan in intend to fish a husband.

One day, as she stands at the roadside, she sees a young man arriving with a small delivery truck and she jumps so that she provokes a small accident.

So, she makes the acquaintance with the 23-year old beautiful Sicilian Domenico Turiano, that looks exactly just like the singer and tenor Domenico Modugno (* 9.1.1928 in Polignano at Mare, Italy; † 6.8.1994 on Lampedusa, Italy).

According to statements of Agnese, she something spoken to in the year 1951 of Claudio Pica and something photographed, at young photographer, who became later famous than Italian singer Claudio Villa, (* 1.1.1926 in Rome, Italy; † 7.2.1987 in Padua, Italy).

He confessed her, that he falls in love with her was and that he wants to marry her.

Agnese refused his proposal of marriage (officially because she was engaged ready with Domenico, informally because Claudio was ugly).

(Claudio Pica (Villa) doesn't have experienced something for a luck he it has had that Agnese has refused him.
If she had accepted his proposition, then would be determined Claudio Villa downfall been.)

Between August and Octobers 1951, Agnese gave herself sexually to the young Domenico, after she had let him in suspense long time.

Short time later, Domenico had to back to Sicily because of the flood-catastrophe, and Agnese find out that she was pregnant.

With a letter, Domenico did clear Agnese that he will only come back if a boy will born.

Agnese was desperate.

She must have to receive a boy at any price. She is even be willing to sell her own soul…

1951
Agnese Vittoria Fioraso

● ● ● ● ● ● ● ● ● ● ●

Angeblich sollte von Claudio Pica (Villa) fotografiert, gerahmt und als Liebesbeweis an Agnese geschenkt.

Allegedly should photograph from Claudio Pica (Villa), framed and given as love-proof at Agnese.

The embryonic-stage (1951-1952)

Agnese went into a nunnery-abbey of a Catholic hospital in Milan and
asked for asylum.
The Mother Superior granted Agnese asylum and promised, that the
doctors would help her to give birth to a male baby.
In return, she promised, the whole pregnancy-time disguises as novice to
be helpful, and that she would say nothing about the many questionable
experiments, for her life a long time.
A questionable medical treatment was also that women, who wanted to
have children, but could not receive, they became inject a liquid, that
which as beer called.
It was claimed that it is about urine of pregnant women, but it was the
rumor that it would be urine of pregnant cows.

The time passed and the spring came, Agnese became ever stouter, the
true novices started to whisper.
It was no longer possible, to hide, that she was pregnant.
Therefore, she was insulated.

End of May 1952, it was so wide, Agnese bore a baby.
But the experiment was abortive, Agnese bore no boy and also no girl
but a mixture from both.
The baby looked like a beautiful girl.
The hormone determining was unequivocally female, it had inner female
organs, but also an unambiguous male organ and suffered at
depression.

The diagnosis of the doctors was:
Hermaphroditic with female determining and chronically depressive ill
feeling, on the basis of the hermaphroditic.
From medical points of view, the doctors recommended an operative
distance of the male organ.
So, the baby would have led a normal life as girls and later than woman
also even children can bear.
But the doctors were bound the hands.
Then they were extorted by Agnese, they were forced to remove the
female organs operationally.

**The Gods could not understand this injustice, therefore they gave
the baby some abilities and took it under their personal protection.**

Despite all, Agnese wanted to know nothing about this baby and refused to acknowledge it.

In the birth certificate-book from the year 1952 – Part I, series A, No. 277, was done following entry:

{In the year 1952, at the 30. May, at 9:20 o'clock, Mr. Vendico Luigi has himself gone to by the signed leader of the registry office of the community Milan, Prof. Arliade Pigó, 42 years old, servant office, resident in Milan, that – from the management of the circle-clinic "Presidio Ospedaliero Macedonio Melloni – Azienda Ospedaliera Fatebenefratelli e Oftalmico" from Milan authorizes, in front of the witness: Francia Luigi, 61 years old, son of the Bassano, porter, resident in Milan and Ghianda Rinaldo, 60 years old, son of the Luigi, resident in Milan, porter - Mr. Vendico Luigi has give following explanation:

"At the 28. May 1952, at 13:40 o'clock, in the house No. 52 the Macedonio-Melloni-Street, is a child been born, his mother not wants recognized.

The child is male gender."

The child, who was not introduced to me, about his birth I make sure me on the basis of the hospital-papers, I have given him the name Walter and the surname FROLETTI.

On my ordinance, the child was brought of Mr. Vendico – that I has handed over the copy of this document for the leader of the institute – the provincial institute for the protection and the welfare of the child "Istituto Provinciale di Protezione ed Assistenza all'Infanzia (IPPAI)" (orphanage).

The present document is signed, after lecture from all present.}

The stolen childhood (1952-1959)

Shortly after the birth, the baby Walter lives for at least 3-6 months in the orphanage in Milan "Istituto Provinciale di Protezione ed Assistenza all'Infanzia (IPPAI)" as not wanted child.

At the 15. November 1952 Domenico married Agnese.
Agnese had withheld Domenico that Walter suffered from hermaphroditic.
After the marriage-rite Agnese attempted to kill the baby, for the first time. She gave Walter a big confectionery.
The grandma saw that the baby was shortly before to the suffocation. She responded quickly. With a finger, she extracted the confectionery.

Then Walter lived alternate with the grandparents, but it became ever showier that it was a girl. It carried long blond hair and was beautiful, but still suffered at depressions.

Agnese wanted to protect the secret at all costs, therefore she induced that Walter was get rid of into a nunnery in the province of Como, where lived orphan-infants until about the age from 7 years. There, there were also several medicine-students.

Since Walter became more and more strikingly, because it played together with other girls with dolls, was induced, that it was treated with electro-shocks, drug-tea and other psychopharmacological, in order to enforce the brain-washings.
These questionable treatments exacerbated only the whole problem. Walter not knew more, who or what it was. As soon as it had fallen asleep, the nightmares started and with the time became more and more badly and bewildered. It had fear of the dark, each night woke up crying and fully hotly-coldly bathed, often it had also sleep-wandered.
Therefore, it became transferred into a room together with a student, because the students have often studied the whole night.

Some of these confusing nightmares that Walter could not understand if was about memories or whether they are pure imaginations, were:

▶ *As observer sees it in an operating room, as doctors at a baby out-operate the female organs and it knows, that the baby is itself. It sees too a nun, who looks like Agnese, that she itself refused to acknowledge the baby and has left it.*

▶ *It falls and falls again and again, into a bottomless and spiral-shaped hole* – (at first, because it has screamed loudly and was awakened, had the pitfall an end, until the next nightmare came).

▶ *On the one side, Walter sees itself as approximately 18-year old girl with antiquated clothes in the 18. or 19. Century in an old convent, where young girls vanished mysterious manner* – (is that one reminiscence at a former life?).
On the other side, it sees itself as small boy of approximately 5-6 years in a modernized part of the convent in the year 1957-1958, where a night is wakened by loud noise. The nuns, children and students were fleeing. Walter fell asleep again. As the after day, as it woke up, was surprised, that all was so quiet. The building lay crooked like the tower of Pisa and no human being was there. Shortly after it, all came back.
(Although both sides have some differences, it is unequivocally about the same place, only in one other century, and in the time, since Walter was in this convent, there was really an earthquake).

▶ Another from such nightmares was also:
Walter was and became ever more curious. It suspected that this convent hid an evil secret and that wanted it to find.
At first, it explored the allowed, then the forbidden areas of the convent. It found a spiral staircase in a tower.
In direction downward, it found a door that belonged to a big vault-cellar. It opened it a split in order to look what was in there.
The room and the persons were very mysterious, it looked like a mass-room, but no normal, but there were celebrated unequivocally black mass and these Satan-worshippers were just about to be sacrificed a baby.
For Walter was a shock. It could not understand what it had just seen and what that had to seek in one Catholic convent.

Approximately in the year 1958, Walter came in Comasina a quarters in Milan to the parents Agnese and Domenico.
Meanwhile, Agnese bore two further children, Elena in the year 1953 and Angelo in the year 1955, and further at least two abortions.
Since Domenico worked as independent scrap-dealer with a small delivery truck, and therefore not sufficiently money earned, the family Turiano was depended on the helps of socially-welfare and relationship.

Agnese hated Walter. She saw it, as it is a deformed creature, a mood of the nature, the ruin of her life.

Part-time she sold it for sex-plays to older children-rapists, for example an old man, the father of a woman Irma.
Agnese was full from hate. Once even, She has thrown down Walter of a stairwell, in the hope, that it dies.
Walter has broken a leg, but it survived. After that, Agnese told that the child was from alone fallen down, during the plays.

Goddess Aphrodite reincarnation (1959-1965)

In the August 1959 as Agnese was in the hospital for to give birth, Walter was to house alone with his approximately 24-year old uncle Vittorio, a beautiful young man with an Apollo-body. Recently time he had come back of the military service and had already fixed the wedding-date with Maria.
Walter had put in his whole female beauty, in order to seduce Vittorio. First, he strived to fight back, but then he could not escape that *"Venus-trap"*. So, a hot love affair began between Walter and Vittorio.

At the 16. August Agnese gave birth to Mimmo. As she came with the baby home, Walter was firm convinced that this newborn is his own child, the fruit of the love affair with Vittorio. He took care of him, so intensively, that Agnese became very annoyed.
She induced that Walter received a therapy with male hormones and told him that that is vitamins.
Walter knew that these injections were no vitamins, but poison for his body. That's why he refused with unbelievable strengths, but against 8-10 men, who held on him, he was powerless.
Walter felt each of these terribly treatments as like the worst rape.
This hormone-therapy could change the blood-values of the child, but not the behavior and also not that *"Dea Aphrodite"* ("Goddess Aphrodite") soul that in this body caught was. Therefore, a baby-doll was bought him, and Walter with the doll get rid of into a children's home in Traona province of Sondrio/Italy, how a troublesome object.
Short time late, of mysterious way, the family Turiano had come to wealth: they possessed suddenly a villa, a big property and a company with at least 10 employees in Arese province of Milan.

(Was maybe this fortune hush-money, respectively blackmail-money or even compensation-money for the abortive experiments?)

The first time in the children's home was very difficult for Walter. Because he played with dolls, constantly the mocking through the other children exposed him. That's why he hid the doll, and so to speak he began a double-life.
► On a side, he was Walter, one completely "more normally", very more intelligently boy. He had the best school-valuations in scientific compartment and was very much interested at technical and electronic appliances, *(it was even the rumor in circulation that he had dismantled a TV and had together-installed again, and the appliance*

had perfectly worked also after it), but in the linguistic compartment (in this case Italian) had very bad school-valuations, so that he had to repeat the second class 3 to 4 times. ◄

► On the other side, it was "Dea Aphrodite", the goddess of the love. She had the talent of the seduction, so that the seduced believed even to be the seducers.
She became very popular and won more and more friends. Her friends felt well in her proximity. Be in sorrow and problems, she was asked for advice, she could console everyone and always had ready the matching advice.
She felt oblige to protect the nature, animals and the defenseless.
Once, as she had to find out, that a friend was sexually abused from the confessor, she put in her charm, in order to lure the priest into the sex-trap. This happened without much effort.
After that, she had all tells, (in the form of jokes).
The issue was hushed up ***(the Vatican is the biggest expert such affair to hold secretly)***, but short time late was the confessor no more to see, and also in the children's home-school was no more priests and sisters (Nuns, similarly home-personnel) appointed, but only came teachers from outside. ◄

Essentially, Walter had a good life in this children's home. He had many friends, what very popular and there something the meals good and sufficiently, and as he noticed, that the nuns ate like "God in France", he has intercepted the meal of the nuns and has organized eat-parties with his friends. The nuns have never get caught him.

But there were also some experiences that have brought Walter to the reflection over the methods of the Catholicism.
For example it gave a friend, who was suffering from a heart condition.
His mother, although she was destitute, on all Sundays came on foot of Milan about her child to visit.
In the time, as Walter was in this children's home, this friend was already officially twice as dead explained and been already put in an open coffin into a room because of the wake. As a third time happened and he from the dead-person-empire came back, immediately the nuns had to too-nailed the coffin; consequently the nuns had pronounced the death sentence and had executed, for this child.
The child received mortal agony. He has screamed loudly and tried to free himself from the death trap, but against the representative of the Vatican, he was powerless.
The nuns took care of it that Walter and the other children left the room and have locked up the room, so that nobody could purely more.

The Sunday after it, as the mother of the dead came, in order to see her son, became her the refuses and the poor woman was told in cold blood, that the child was be dead and she was simply thrown out.
Walter could not forget the death-screams, but he noticed, that he possessed the talent to see the sundries and to communicate with them. He promised his dead friend, that he would take care of it to make known the circumstances of his death, and so to provide to take care of it, that the soul of this good friend can find its peace again.

(At the latest after the publication of this book, the Justice-goddess will take carry that this murder is uncovered and is exhumed the corpse of this soul. The remains of the coffin will prove, that the child has still lived as the coffin was too nailed.)

In the whole time, as Walter was in this children's home, Agnese had visited him only one single time.
In contrast to it, his father Domenico came each time since he was commercially in the proximity. That was two to three times per month.

In the year 1962, as Walter was ten years old, he spent the school vacations at home. One day, he was quite alone with Agnese in the villa, as a long limousine with darkened panes halted before the family-property.
The driver opened the back door of the car, in order to be a nun helpful when getting off. At the same moment, Walter saw, that an eminence of the Vatican-family in the red habit sat beside the nun.
Agnese said Walter that the nun, whose name was Agnese too, is a cousin, who extra from Rome had arrived, in order to get to know Walter. Walter had mixed feelings opposite this nun, who was unequivocally much older than Agnese, and too had a stunning similarity with Agnese. On the one hand, he felt very strongly attracted; but on the other hand was here very strongly refusing and despising feelings.
The memory at his own birth ran like a film before his eyes.

Was the nun Agnese his true naturally mother, who had immediately left him after the birth?
Was the eminence that sat in the limousine, possibly even his true naturally fathered?
Which nun leaves drives herself in a limousine from Rome to Milan, accompanies from an eminence, only in order to visit one sole ten-year cousin?

As Walter was approximately thirteen years old, Domenico decided, against the will Agnese that the child came to Arese to the family and went there also to the school.
At one of the last days in the children's home, as Walter wanted to say goodbye to his best friends, became conscious him, that he was simultaneously engaged with ten boys.
He knew that was loved very much, but at the same time with ten? That was him at first really conscious, as he wanted to say goodbye.

The realization (1965-1967)

The day came, that Walter should definite leave the children's home in Traona.
It was beautiful weather and Walter was been cheerfully. Domenico had picked him up with the delivery truck, but ever near they Arese came, Walter became all the sadder. The terribly memories at his birth and the first eight years of his life came back.
He knew, as soon as he in the "at home" had arrived; he was *"the black witch"* Agnese delivered.
He fell into the acute depression and as he arrived at home, he was already badly sick, with high fever. The doctor was helpless; only Agnese knew, but she was not ready to betray "the secret".

Not until as Walter lived in Arese, he met his brothers and sister Elena, Angelo and Mimmo. He became conscious itself, that they actually really know themselves only since approximately three years and only in the vacation time had seen *(did on purpose Walter be kept away by the brothers and sister?)*
Walter knew only that "brother" Mimmo *("the fruit of the love affair with Vittorio")* and also could not forget, how Mimmo shortly after his birth was at the bed bound with many hoses for the infusions in the hospital, because of a poisoning *(supposedly, the mother's milk of Agnese was not perfect)*. It went and lives or death.

A few years later, Elena and Angelo were pushed off into a children's home and came home only in the vacations.
Short time later, Agnese had pushed through, that again Walter was pushed into the children's home, to Thiene province of Vicenza, where Elena and meanwhile also Mimmo were. Actually, it was an institute for children, that insane, physically handicapped, thalidomide-catastrophe-babies and that of the Dioxin-accident in Seveso in North-Italy. This children's home be in charged of from nuns.
But this time, Walter didn't play along, he went in the hunger strike with immediate effect and threatened in the case, that he is not sent home again, he would vanish within two weeks. Look there, after about ten days he was picked up.

Walter lived in Arese circa two years. It seemed first as if would be in the family of everything in order, but the appearance tarnished.
Came Walter nightmares and the somnambulism more and more frequently. He started to ask questions.

Agnese attempted first to avoid the questions, but Walter had not to let up and asked again and again. Therefore, Agnese had occurred itself fairy-tales that it became always contradicting and implausible.
Since the first name Walter was very rare in Italy, he wanted to know why he had been named so. Agnese claimed that was the first name from an ex-fiancé from Padua.
Walter always had a strong suspicion that he had been done as baby by an operation to the one boy (after all the nightmares must have a meaning). Therefore he looked for proof and sees there; in the shame-area he found (hardly visible) scars.
He strived to receive an explanation of Agnese. First, she tried to ignore him, and then she told (in a behavior und stress, the Walter already from her knew, if she lied and tried to hush up something); that he has immediately been operated after the birth at a hernia.
The suspicion, that Agnese was not his natural mother (despite strong similarity) became ever stronger, (which natural mother tries to betray her own child, to sell, to tell lies to him, to poison, to murder and to take advantage of him?).

For a long time Walter had noticed ready, that Agnese was a chronic liar and therefore completely implausible. But she drank wine very gladly (…and as an antiquated saying goes: "The truth is in the wine"). Walter made use of that in order to experience the truth.

If Agnese had drunk a few glassfuls of wine, Walter received some confirmations about his suspicions, under others following:
► He experienced that the "person" that had born him, the whole pregnancy-time over as nun disguises had spent in a nunnery, that she wanted necessarily to give birth a boy, that during the birth was ascertained deformities and that "corrections" had taken place.
► … she has a cousin, the nun is and that she is called Agnese too.
► … until he was about six years old was in a nunnery near Como. In this time, there was also an earthquake.
► … and many others of Agnese secrets.
As Agnese was sober again, Walter confronted she with her statements, but she has denied everything and claimed, that he is a liar and he would have one flourishing fantasy.
At the latest now, Walter was sure, that the nightmares are true memories.
Walter makes clear Agnese, that he knew the truth, that she is unreliable and that he doesn't believe that she is his mother.

The "apparent undamaged" family-lives of the Turiano started to shatter. At each opportunity Agnese had Walter sensed, that she hated him.

She tried continuously to provoke him, so that he beat her, in order to have a reason, to push him again and finally into a children's home. But however Walter ignored her simply and treated her as she would be air, but with a certain caution, that he knew, that Agnese was his worst enemy.

(Whoever has Agnese as friend, wife, relatives respectively as mother then he (she) needs no enemy!)

In these times, started with Walter the first suicide-thoughts. He decided, at the latest with twenty-one years, to do a leaving of this world, but that the situation became more and more intolerably, he tried it already earlier.

With the time, Walter ascertained, that he had also the talent, to make itself invisibly, or even with his "astral-bodies", to travel to other worlds.

Walter used this talent, in order to escape from such situations. He vanished for hours, often even for days (without the family-property too abandoned). Even search operations were done, but even if he was in the view-area nobody could see him (or nobody wanted to see him?). Even if he itself procured something to meals in the kitchen during Agnese the dishes washed off, he was not seen.

Agnese tried everything possible, in order to subjugate Walter, even before "the black magic" didn't stop she. She embezzles a tooth of Walter during a tooth-treatment, about to use for a black ceremony.

The Gods had foreseen also that and that's why they had equipped Walter with a protection-coat that it likes a shield all negative radiations reflected back to the sender.

Agnese tried Walter to persuade, that the children their parents, particularly the mother "<u>always and blindly</u>" believes and trusts "<u>must</u>", that the children "<u>only</u>" would be there, in order to subsidize financially the parents particularly in the age, and that they "<u>would have to</u>" their parents "<u>on each case</u>" honors and respects.
On the other hand, ready Walter made her clear, that belief, trust, honor and respect, one had would first to earn themselves, and "<u>before</u>" one rights receives, "<u>must</u>" one first obligations fulfils.

Shorter time late, oddly enough Walter happened an accident, as he wanted from the kitchen into the cellar down. The ladder slip from his

feet away and he fell. In the same moment, Domenico entered the room (he was unexpected arrive to house).
Agnese responded lightning and immediately caught the arm of Walter, therefore to prevent the worst with him.

(Had Agnese tried again to kill Walter, and him only in last second rescued, because she wanted none witness? – That the ladder was so fast, that actually no accident should happen.)

Agnese started to make Walter badly. She told everywhere, that Walter was being spiteful and other lies. Even uncle Pierino (Pietro) believed her, without to ask Walter's versions (after all each medal has two sides), and he to slap Walter's face in two different cases.
Agnese tried to convince Domenico, Walter again and for always to get rid of, but Domenico refused and placed itself on Walter's side.

Agnese turned the skewer and made Domenico the life to the hell. She refused the matrimonial duties. She served over-salt meals. She provoked him lasts to fighting and so on.
Well yes, the poor Domenico remained nothing other, as goes strangely, in order to gratify his sexual-needs, where he also received decently to the meal and he had his peace before Agnese. But he has not beaten her one single time, also not, as she has thrown him behind the espresso-machine fully with cooking coffee.
In few years, Agnese had reached, that Domenico lost everything and bankruptcy had to announce.
Domenico separated from Agnese, that she was unbearable him.

In a time, that Walter lived and worked with Domenico together, told Domenico him some "family secrets" under other following:
▶ As he was a young man, as the war came to an end, Mussolini's elites had arrested four different men and forced to transport two coffin-form heavy boxes to a particular hiding place, and there to bury.
Domenico carried the fore box. As the rear box fell and shattered, one of the men said: "That is precious metal!"
After completion of the secret-mission, to the appearance, the men were freed, but as Domenico conscious became, that in retrospect the others three men died at secretly full "accidents", immediately he left the region Latium by Rom and that has probably rescued his life.

(Walter could not recognize, if this history is true or untrue, but strangely, shortly after it, all Italian media spoke about "Mussolini's treasure", also the lawyer Moschella, a cousin of Domenico, that his

office in Milan had, he was burning interested, to experience the
secret and therefore he tried to interrogate Walter.)

► Domenico told about the suspicion, that the grandpa Luigi, the father
of Agnese, possibly in the year 1958 was poisoned.
(Interesting is, that still ten years after his death, his corpse during
the shifting, still almost unscathed and mould-green was, an
unambiguous symptom one arsenic poisoning!)
It was also the rumor, that the second man of grandma Maria Luigia the
mother of Agnese, his first wife had thrown from balcony and so that she
came to death.

► Domenico told Walter too, that he a sealed cover for him has
deposited at the police-presidency of Milan. In this cover stands the
whole "truth" about Walter "origin" and it should be handed over to him,
as soon as he will of age.

(Strangely, short time after it, Agnese had reached, that Domenico
came into a lunatic asylum and a brainwashing received. The cover
that Domenico had deposited at the police-presidency vanished
without a trace.)

Domenico & Agnese

Circa 1965

Take flight (1967-1969)

The family-court had withdrawn Agnese and Domenico from the parent's custody.
That Elena, Angelo and Mimmo were already in the children's home, the problem was, what should happen with the already about 15-16-year old Walter?
During the custody-process, Walter was asked about his opinion.
He made unequivocally clear, that he would rather live on the streets, than to go into a home again or with that "parents" to live, and already not at all with Agnese!
The youth-judge on the other hand explained him, that that would not be possible, that the Italian state is responsible for him.
He promised Walter, that he will order an accommodation in a boarding school in Milan, where he has his total freedom on the day, but in the evening must be back. There, he would have at least one secure housing with board and lodging at public expenses.
The judge asked Walter, himself to be patient a few months, until a place becomes free and he should as long as still lives with Agnese.

It turned one of the longest and worst times in Arese, in the Walter completely alone and helplessly Agnese delivered was.
Unfortunately, his good friend and bodyguard had died since short, a sheepdog of name Bobby, that him always and everywhere accompanies and protected had, that even, as Walter was in the school, on him had waited in front of the school-building.
His therapist Bianca, a snow-white cat, that him mental assistance during his depressive phase gave, had vanished without a trace for months.

Thanks are the Gods, that at the time he had a job in a small repair-workshop for precious-clocks and precious-jewelry in a side street of the Turin-Street in the center Milan. There was not much money, but it has been enough for the tickets and for the lunches, and he had peace of Agnese for about ten hours on the day.

The time passed and it became always more and more unbearable.
Walter decided to vanish without a trace, if soon didn't come message from the youth-judge.

About five months had passed since the custody-process, as a Sunday in the morning two police appeared with a warrant of arrest against

Walter. They could not justify the arrest, that them no one piece of information was available.
In the youth-prison of Milan, Walter asked for a conversation with the prison-director and explained him the error.
The director had no doubts about Walter's sincerity. He transferred him into a room with only another prisoner, he offered him a trust-activity in the kitchen and promised, with the judge to speak, because of the error.

Later, Walter experienced, that the nice young man, who lived in the room at the attic of the youth-prison with him, nobody other as the famous nobleman-burglar was, that before leaving the scenes of the crime the ladies of the house sexually masturbated. For this reason the burglaries were often not reported.

He offered Walter to take him along, as he planned the escape over the roof of the prison, but Walter had to refuse for two reasons; firstly, because he was not free from dizziness and secondly, because he didn't want to be on the escape, a life long, for mistakes, that he had not committed.

About six months were passed again, as even Walter planned intellectually the escape over the kitchen-suppliers-door, as finite the judge-date came.
It was the same judge. Walter seemed to him known, however the judge knew no longer, about what it went.
It was Walter that him the memory had to freshen.
After checkup of Walter's statements the judge apologized and promised as soon as possible transfer in the boarding school.
Walter made clear to him, that he had no patience more and in the case, that the issue would not be taken care of in a short time, then he definite vanishes and the judge carries the full responsibility for it.
After about two weeks Walter was transferred in the boarding school in Torrazza-Street number 80, in the Gallaratesse quarter of Milan.

The boarding school was established and was leading from three men:
► One was a beautiful man, who was responsible for the legal issues and for the administration of the cash values from which boarding school-inhabitants. He did no secret from it, that he was a homosexual with a preference for blood-young boys.
One of morning early, as Walter rang at his door, because he required some money; he was bathed in sweat with only one panties dresses, and a stark naked, blood-young at best 15-year old boy was just came out of his bedroom.

▶ The second was one somewhat stouter man with a handicap in walking, which was responsible for the boarding school-administration and for the sale of canteen-vouchers too.
Always Walter had an odd feeling, if he was near this inconspicuous man. He was confident, that he had to do it with a criminal, but didn't come first behind it, what was wrong. At fist, as Walter was already several years no longer there, he experienced the truth.

▶ Don Abramo was the third and eldest man. He was responsible for the souls.
He must be a true saint, because there was only kindness to hear over him. Walter had use its whole *"Dea Aphrodite's skill"*; in order to seduce Don Abramo, but it remained without success.
An evening in a bar, Walter won a blue ceramics-jug, fully with Mexican Tequila. He drank everything up and went back in the boarding school. He went into the office of Don Abramo, gave him the empty jug, undressed stark naked and danced on the desk.
Don Abramo remained completely calm and didn't make use of the situation, gave Walter a few Espressos and as he was somewhat sober again, he accompany him to the sleep-room.
On the day after it, Walter was perplexed. Despite the heavy alcohol-consumption, he had suffered no poisoning and Don Abramo was the first man, Man, who could resist him sexually.

The time in the boarding school took its course; Walter received his job again in the small repair-workshop for precious-clocks and precious-jewelry. In the evening, he tried to do the leaving certificate for secondary-modern-school in the evening-school.
An evening in the year 1968, as he did homework, while the festival of Sanremo ran in the TV, he heard a deeper voice that sang a song that a woman should sing.
Walter looked to the TV and saw fully surprise Patty Bravo (* 9.4.1948 in Venice, Italy; actually Nicoletta Strambelli), a twenty-year-old Italian pop-singer, the fully doll-fuller eroticism sang (only the voice disturbed. The voice was unequivocally male), "La Bambola" (the doll).
Walter immediately recognized, that he possibly had another a chance, the physical damages, that Agnese had caused him, one day somewhat to can, has repaired.

At weekends and at holidays, Walter went, most of all on foot in order to save money, to the children's home in Baggio a quarters in Milan, in order to visit the three-year-younger brother Angelo, and if he had sufficiently money for the trip to the children's home in Thiene, province of Vicenza, then he visited his sister Elena and the youngest brother Mimmo.

Once in August he granted himself a trip to Santa Teresa of Riva, province of Messina, in order to visit the relationship on the father's side. He was received heartily, but problems occurred soon. Walter contorted with his feminine behavior the heads of the village-men, the women saw him as threat.

The aunts prohibited him, the house too leaved, but he didn't let himself pleased that.

The mayor became, from his own wife, under pressure put down, so that he was forced, to give Walter village-prohibition, because he was so-called too scandalous.

Walter could not understand, why such a theater was done, after all no people being had complained in Milan over his feminine type. The opposite was the case.

Anyway, it went with Walter uphill. He received the hope, to have the possibility soon, to have operated him to the woman back, and consequently his personality development, to leave her free sprint. The hope faded, as he noticed through coincidence, that Agnese, behind his back at Don Abramo, her wrong compassion-tour played.

Walter made unequivocally clear, that through court-decision Agnese no rights at him had. Therefore she had to let him alone and was not allowed to interfere herself in his life, that she was undesirable.

Since the day, everything went downhill again.

One day, the aunt Carmelina (Carmela), the youngest sister of Domenico, came from Sicily, and asked Walter to be helpful you with the work-quest.

Walter was too naive and took itself a few days free.

Several weeks later, Walter lost his work-position. As reason the employer declared, that Agnese had called constantly and if Walter was not present, also in the company appeared, in order to excite pity.

Domenico that was released from the lunatic asylum for months visited Walter and introduced his German friend Hildegard Haetzel. Domenico did Walter the offer, if he agreed, that he applies the custody for him and for him will take care. Walter assumed with joys, but only, if nothing more to do to have with Agnese.

A week later, Domenico had, in the presence and with consent of Walter, in presence of the socially-helper in the youth welfare department the custody-papers signed.

Short time after it, Agnese had induced, that Domenico landed in the lunatic asylum again.

Was the socially civil servant the traitress, the Agnese about the custody-proposition had informed?

Hildegard, that spoke hardly Italian, and no had help to expect from the German consulate, Walter asked for help at the sale of her expensive jewelry.
Walter had advised them then, the whole beautiful and expensive jewelry not to sell, but only a minor small gold-necklace. This had been sufficient completely for the return trip to Berlin, and consequently the loss in limited held.
Through this advice, good friends became Hildegard and Walter.
Hildegard went back to Berlin, and as Walter noticed, that still Agnese spies him after, he definitive leaves the boarding school and lived from then on in the Confalonieri-Street opposite the tax-office-ministry of Milan. It was a small room with leaky roof, where Domenico had lived penultimate.

In the same year, in the autumn-winter 1968, the on the father's side grandmother died, Domenico received free-days for the lunatic asylum, in order to take part in the burial of his mother, in Sicily.
Immediately after the funeral, Domenico immigrated to Berlin to Hildegard, and therefore he could definite escape from Agnese.

In the winter 1968-1969 Walter went very badly. The small room was icy-cold, Money for meals didn't available and already not at all for the fuel. Three different very poor and old neighbors; a woman that had flat foots as hindrance; a female teacher, who was for a long time retired; and a man, that himself with a job as car-park-guard held over water; they brought Walter, although they themselves had nothing, again and again a soup and if they knew, where it a few dough to earn gave, then they immediately told him.
Without the three generous neighbors, Walter would have the winter definitely doesn't survive.

The spring came, as the authorities received wind of it, that the building in the Confalonieri-Street was collapse-endangered; the inhabitants were necessary-evacuated into the adjacent building.
Walter came into a room with other boys, where there were only need-beds.
In the same afternoon, suddenly and undesirable Agnese appeared. She used from Walter's naivety and kind-heartedness and claim that she would have no place to sleeping for the night.

Walter could her whining no longer hear. Therefore he said to her, that
she could sleep only one single night in the room, where he himself had
slept until the day before it, but she must be quietly and could not leave
the room until the day after it, that a prohibition covers became for the
night.
On the day after it, Walter regretted that. Agnese had taken advantage of
his good faith, all searches and some objects lets vanish. As Walter took
her to task, she denied and had still the insolence to try, to extort him,
with the argument, that he let she there slept, although it was prohibited;
if he doesn't claim opposite the authorities, that Agnese there already
since some time together with him lived had.
Walter immediately threw out her, and said that she should herself
ashamed and that she could still to report him. She will just feel, whoever
will pull the shorter.

**Who had informed Agnese about the need-evacuation, and wanted
she with the blackmail attempt to an apartment reaches, because
she lived ready for a long time in a pension?**

Some weeks later, a Mr. Vito Ratano appeared, an engineer of Alfa
Romeo in Milan. Walter had seen him already once, as the property of
the Turiano was auctioned because of bankruptcy.
He could not take the estate in the property, if the previous possessor
Domenico had not evacuated it previously, and an action for eviction
would have lasted years.
Walter explained himself willing to mediate in writing with Domenico, but
he could give no success-guarantee.

Walter was somewhat bewildered, as few days late Mr. Ratano again
there was, but Vito explained him kindly, that he would have spoken with
his wife over his situation, and if he agreed, then he wants to help him, to
look for another apartment and a work. Walter accepted the help-offers.
That Walter was still underage, the help-willingness proved to be
somewhat complicated, but inter-solutions could be found.

On the ninth July, Walter could start as apprentice in the Metal–and
Mechanical Engineering- Businesses LA. ME. PRE. s.r.l., that later had
moved to the number 43 in the Negrotto-Street, and a small room was
found for him in the Gian-Battista-Grassi-Street in the quarters Roserio,
not far from the job.

Meanwhile, Domenico had agreed the evacuation, the former property.
Unfortunately, the sale of the factory-machines brought not much that it

was sell only as scrap metal, but so the Ratano could take their ownership in property.

Walter regarded the Ratano as his family that he in truth only an on paper had had.
The Ratano reported Walter that they knew a family with small children that would have liked to adopt the sister Elena, that she should take care of the children, but only if Walter agreed.
Walter on the other hand said, although he had nothing against it and also he was the oldest of the brothers and sister. He didn't intend however to dictate they, what they to do would have. That's why the offer should become done directly to Elena, that only something her wanted is important.
Elena accepted the offer and came in Milan to the new adoption-family that was a few minutes removed from Walter's room. Later, the Ratano wanted also to help, that also the brother Mimmo could get to Milan, maybe even in the children's home in Baggio, where the brother Angelo was.

Anyway, one could think, that it from this time for Walter again uphill went.
At the work there were no problems and he was accepted as he was, also in his other surroundings the people were kindly to him.
Least once per week, he went to visit Angelo, and he could see Elena even almost every day; but where the sun seems there are also many shadows.

Over a spy in the youth-office, Agnese had find out the new address of Elena.
She forced Elena to hand over from Walter's address and started again to terrorize him.
Walter tried, Agnese cold-blooded terrorism, from the way to go, but she doesn't let up and waylaid him constantly.

To the suicide and emigrating driven (1969-1970)

The autumn 1969, although cold and so foggily, that one the fog with a knife could cut, became known as the hot autumn of Milan, because lasts general-strike gave and the people very much has demonstrated. Definitely, Walter would have survived also this bad time, if Agnese had let him alone.
He fell into acute depressions again.

On Monday, that tenth November, because he saw no more way out, and about definite from Agnese in peace to be left, he decided to do suicide. He cooked a soup with one-liter strong bleaches and he forced himself to eat everything.

But the Gods were not yet ready to call Dea Aphrodite in Olympus back.

It was an agonizing night, but Walter had survived it. He remained another day in bed that he was not capable to get up.
On Wednesday, he decided to emigrate; therefore to escape from Agnese, he collected his last strength and got himself inquiry over price, time and whether his personal identification card was valid for West-Berlin Germany.
On Thursday, he quit his job at the LA. ME. PRE.
As reason he declared, that a cousin from Rome him had offered, with him to live and to work.
With this white lie, Walter wanted to hold the emigration secretly.

The wage, for the last ten working days, would have been enough for the ticket to West Berlin, if necessary also for the return journey.
On Friday the fourteenth, Walter vanished without a trace from Milan, without to say goodbye.

He spent the journey in a nonsmoker-compartment, alone with a nice, pretty and helpful young Italians, who were a few years older than he. After short time, the two approached, and so Walter could forget for a few hours, that he four days before still on the threshold of the death lay. Shortly before the border of the GDR (German Democratic Republic), the boy got out.

The GDR's passport officials made use of that Walter spoke no single word German, and therefore they plundered his last money. They had taken an important decision from Walter with it.
Walter knew, that a journey was now without return and he in West Berlin had to remain, whether he wanted or not.

On Saturday the fifteenth November against eighteen o'clock, Walter arrived at the railway station West Berlin-Zoological Garden. He wanted to visit Domenico and Hildegard, that he knew, that they were every Saturday evening at the parents of Hildegard.
He went to the taxi rank and showed the taxi-driver a note with the address of Hildegard's parents in the district Wedding, near to the Miller-Street.

There, Walter showed the old man, who opened the door, photography on the Domenico with Hildegard was to see.
Hildegard was called.
She received him with big joy and paid the taxi-driver. As Domenico Walter saw, he almost received a heart attack and was, for several hours, not in the situation to speak.

Walter asked Domenico, to be helpful him to look for a work and apartment, and volunteered as soon as like possible to pay back the extended money.
First, Domenico was not ready, but then he has altered his opinion and agreed to be helpful.
The first night slept Walter in the heated garden-arbor, but as on the day after it known became, that was prohibited in the winter, he was quartered again in the house.

Domenico had held his word, and also with Hildegard help, became anxiously for him that of stay–and work approval.
A room was found in the district Zehlendorf, as roomer at an old retired actress; and on the twentieth-eight November he could start to work at the company Stamp-Freiberg in the Federal-Avenue 214, where also Domenico worked.
Already after the first month-pay, Walter could pay back his debts with Domenico.

The hippie-times (1970-1976)

The 70er year, the so-called hippie-times, was for Walter almost like one benediction.
He could his true feminine side, nearly completely life it up, without to attract attention. He let himself grow the hair, wore very tight pants, extravagant blouses, Shoes with high heels, Furs from rabbit-fur and so on.
The people believed, that he was a hippie, only his friends and the persons, who knew him long, knew respectively the truth suspected.

With Domenico, he got things straight already after some months. With a so-called "Conversation between father and son" he made clear to him, that he loved only men.
Domenico was confused. It seemed, that he would remember what, but could not remind. He was not in the situation, to tell something.
Since this conversation, the two saw themselves more and more rarely and the relationship was rather tense. That's why Walter had must give up, the occupation at the company Stamp-Freiberg after about three months. Shortly after it, Domenico started to work as electrician at the AEG Berlin-Wedding.

The brainwashing, that Domenico received in the lunatic asylum, had been thorough, he had forgotten most and had to learn much again.
For example he had beginning of the seventies-years, as he worked at the AEG, shown plan-drawings at Walter over an electric train that only on a rail could drive.
Domenico was solidly confident, that he would have invented him from short; but Walter could remember exactly, that already him many years before from him similar had been shown, in the time in Arese, where he together with him lived and had worked.

The small room, in Berlin-Zehlendorf, it could heat only with one camping stove, therefore it was very moist.
The old actress lived together with her nephew, who were at least fifty year younger; and likely they has have almost each night sex together, that was unlikely, that the two last jumps on the bed has done.
That Walter's room lay beside it, he could not often sleep.
The old lady accused Walter the theft of a wrong diamond-ring, that how it was missing also again had been found.

In January or February of the year 1970 Walter moves to a worker-
hostel, that earlier was a cloister, in the Schönstedt-Street Berlin-
Wedding, opposite the district court. There he lived for about a half year.

In March, he found a work-position as car-washers for about six weeks at
a DEA-gas-station in Berlin-Wilmersdorf.

End of April, he found through Giovanni, an Italian friend, work at the
textile-company Fritz Marggraff in Berlin-Charlottenburg. There, he
operated the knitter-machine and was there employs until April 1971.

Walter got annoyed every time, as he received the wage that under a
hidden item always a certain percentage shares for church tax him was
withdrawn.
He was of the opinion that such a tax only on voluntary basis should be.
That he was still underage, he asked Domenico for a signature for the
exit from the church.
First, Domenico was against it, but as him clear became, that he could
save taxes so, he signed with joys and a few days later he left the church
too.
The judge asked Walter about the reason of the exit, as he received the
answer: "During my birth, I was not asked, whether I agreed or not!"

In the second half of the year 1970, he received through Domenico a
room-apartment with kitchen and tiled stove, but WC outside the
apartment. It was in a demolition-house in the Ramler-Street 15, in
Berlin-Wedding.

Walter was not yet eighteen, as he had emigrated from Italy, that's why
with appropriate application he could have himself exempt from the
military service.
He was regarded officially as doing social work instead of military service
in the external duty in the foreign countries. So to speak as a sales
representative for Italy, but as such he was allowed to go in Italy only for
about three months per year, and every time he had to apply previously,
until he was thirty years old. And himself every time, in Italy arrived, at
the police reports, that in the case he would have been caught out the
applied time or without police-announcement, then he had to must
imitate the military service.

Walter received the manuscripts for the leading role in the film about
"Jesus Christ" and for the film "In the name of the law", as he had applied
in writing with application-photos at the filmmakers in the film-city
"Cinecittà" at Rome.

For more than six months, he should goes to the film-rehearsals to
Rome. Unfortunately He had to renounce, otherwise the Italian state
would have collected ninety-nine percent of the actor-fee, on the basis of
the military service.

In the spring of the year 1971, Giovanni wanted to marry. Therefore, he
asked Walter, whether he wanted to be his marriage witness in Italy.
Walter assumed with joy.
In April, Walter can be driven with Giovanni's sport car in the Tuscany, at
the first times after the escape and against the wills of Agnese.
Unfortunately, Walter could not function as marriage witness, that he was
still underage. But substitute could be found.
After some days, he goes by train first to Thiene in order to visit Mimmo;
then to Milan, where he first lived in a pension. After some days, he was
guest at a young man, who had learned to know him in the cinema in the
Turin-Street. There he remained, until he went back to Berlin again.

During a meeting with Elena and Angelo at aunt Silvana, Agnese was
present too.
Agnese had appeared without dentures, therefore to excite compassion
to Walter. She claimed, that at her work-position as household-help she
had to work how an animal and received not sufficiently to eat.
Walter already knew this trick. Therefore, he said cold to her, that she
should put her prosthesis into the mouth. Then, one will see, that she
doesn't suffer from malnutrition.
Agnese started, that she could reach nothing, to terrorize Walter again,
so that he was forced, Italy quickly again too abandoned.

Again in Berlin, he ascertained, that he had been quit. He had to stay
above water with unemployment-money or with small jobs, was often
sick and became ever sicker, almost every night the old nightmares
came again and again, that already since his birth and the first eight
years his life pursued.
Again and again he tried to excrete from this life, but unfortunately
without success.

Middle of June he worked for about three weeks at the Gerritvan Delden
& Co in Berlin-Zehlendorf, and from the end of August until middle of
November at the B. Th. Vomachten in Berlin-Spandau, both in the textile-
industry.

In November 1971, on the way to employment office, he was run over by
a rapid taxi-driver and several meters wide hurled. He fell with the head

on the sidewalk. He was written sick over six months because of the
concussion.
First end of May 1972, he could work again. He found a job at Rudolf
Pienn, a store for carpets and curtains in Berlin-Wedding. There, he was
employed until end of February 1973.

In the year 1973, with the oil-boycott, the economic crisis came too, and
with it the short time allowance. Walter received to sense that too and
was until end of July without work. Then, he foundation work until middle
of September 1976 at the textile-company Heinrich Kunert in Berlin-
Marienfeld.

It had to have been at evening in this Time, than in the Italian mission in
Berlin-Wilmersdorf in the near of the subway Uhland-Street, Walter had
learned to know a short and ugly, but very nice man, that introduced
itself as Allan Stewart Konigsberg.
He must have been somewhat younger as forty years old and claimed to
be Woody Allen.
Allan told Walter parts of his history, for example over his partner Mia
Farrow and the dispute because of the twins. He showed even some
newspapers, but at that time Walter could start nothing with the name
"Woody Allen", that up to this time he of him still nothing had heard.
Well yes, however, nevertheless that Allan was not Walter's type, Allan
had made it each time with him to have sex. Like appeared Allan
vanished one day again from Berlin.
Not until year later, Walter saw some films from Woody Allen and
recognized him.

***Maybe only after the publication of this book, one is experienced
whether Allan, that Walter had learned to know at that time, really
Woody Allen was or only one double, and maybe this history is
filmed from Woody Allen.***

In the vacations to Italy, Walter went, although he had a very good
relationship with the brothers and sister, very rare and if yet he tried
Agnese to go from the way, that otherwise it always dispute gave, and he
always in the depression declined, with the consequence that he tried to
kill themselves.
Already for years Angelo knew over Walter's problem and also over
Agnese's nastiness.
Once, he told, that he received given complete equipment from antique
furniture, from a countess of Milan, but he the gift had to refuse, because
Agnese wanted to seize the control.

Although Walter's principle something, "privately and commercial respectively professional, to hold separately", in the year 1975 or 1976 he left himself an on the sexual advances from a superior in the company Heinrich Kunert.
That was a blond and very slim young man from Bavaria. That therefore the work-climate had suffered from it; Walter lost his job.
On the twenty-first September 1976, he found a new work as rough looking at the textile-company wool-manufacture Lorenit in Berlin-Spandau. There, he worked until July 1979.

Despite future-vision, incapable to change
(1976-1978)

October 1976 was ready it. The house, in the Ramler-Street 15 in Berlin-Wedding, should soon is torn off.
Walter found quickly one-room-apartment in the high-rise building in the Candle-Way 1, in Berlin-Spandau, not far from the work-position. At the first November 1976, he could move to there.

Walter noticed soon, that in the new apartment something was not being right. His depressions became more and more worse and with it also the attempted suicides.
He received a new type of visions that him strongly confused, for example:

▶ *A morning he woke up and noticed, that something is not correct. The walls and the floor of the apartment lay crooked.*
He looked from the window and saw, that the high-rise lay crooked and a big crane tried to support it, about consequently it again to put straightly.

▶ *He noticed one day when waking up, that the walls were black from soot. It stank, as a fire has occurred, and the window-openings were to nail shut with boards.*

Walter could not recognize, whether these visions were already last or still will come. Therefore, he asked Lieselotte someone's advice, she was an older neighbor, that already lived there, since shortly after the house-construction.
Lieselotte confirmed, that through an engineer-mistake the house was short before overturning. It was evacuated and with a crane again raised.
Lieselotte confirmed too, that in the time, where a tenant lived in the apartment of Walter, so-called she was a cathouse-mother, that offered her girls to the men for love-services, until on mysterious way a fire happened.

The apartment of Walter lay in the sixth floor and the apartment-number was sixty-six (it were three six, therefore 666). Was that the reason for the strong mystic atmosphere in this apartment?

Walter noticed each time, if surprising he was to visit to Domenico, that
since some time he lived with the newest girlfriend Marianne Margarete
Hohenstein born Noth in Berlin-Moabit, that with the meal that was
already prepared something could not be right.
The meal had been enough definitely also for a third person, but
Marianne insisted each time to that, extra to cook for Walter. Only if he
was announced to the meal, then all ate the same.
Walter's suspicion increased, that Marianne poisoned Domenico slowly,
but he could not prove it.

At the beginning of August 1977, Domenico, that was very sick since
already over one year, and that the doctors could not find why, he asked
Walter for a meeting at a neutral haunt, that the conversation had to take
place only under four eyes.
They even met in the parks Humboldt-grove in Berlin-Wedding near the
AEG.
Domenico told, that he would have the suspicion, since some time slowly
to be poisoned from Marianne.
He also told, that soon he wanted to spend his vacation in Taormina
(Messina), and as soon as he was in Berlin back, absolutely he had to
speak with him, that he had remembered again, what he had
experienced over Walter's birth and the first eight years after it.
Domenico confirmed, that this conversation is very important for Walter.
He would experience, who he real is and a new era would start for him.
Domenico also promised Walter, to support him morally in his new period
of life.

In the night from the Tuesday to the Wednesday, the seventeen August,
Walter received again a new vision.

***Walter saw Domenico in the vision, that tried to murder him through
poison, and he saw how Walter died of it agonizingly.***

As Walter woke up, he was bathed in sweat and totally bewildered, but
he felt himself mysteriously free, and he knew that from immediately his
fate had taken a turn.
In the same evening, he had put on make-up and wore a long evening
dress with a slit that put his right leg to show.
He ordered himself a taxi, in order to go to celebrate.
The taxi-driver was not in the situation to drive straight ahead. A so
beautiful young woman with so nice long legs he had not yet seen. By a
hair's breadth he could still prevent a frontal-accident with a truck.

Admittedly since some years, Walter was known in the "scene" as acquaintance and wardrobe-person of Wolfgang Klein, one over seventy-year old former dancer, who appeared as travesty-artists "Dolly", but in this evening it was the first time, that Walter appeared as full-woman in the public on the stage of the life, and almost all men had the head lost because of this vamp.

Some days later, by telephone Walter received through Angelo the message, that on the seventeen August Domenico was dead because of a poisoning through a dilapidated vanilla-ice.

Was Domenico's poisoning an accidental tragic accident, or a cold-bloody murder? After all Domenico knew exactly, that he was sick and something similar was not allowed eating.

Walter's double-life was no longer a secret. He went to the work as Walter, but as soon as end of work was, she was Dea Aphrodite.

An evening, she loaded Wolfgang Brands, a friend. Dea had received him as vamp.
Wolfgang was completely speechless. He was confident, from Liza Minnelli been received.

Dea spent the New Year's Eve 1977 and the New Year's Night 1978, as paying guest in a saloon, where travesty-artists appeared.
It lay near the Kurfürstendamm in Berlin-Wilmersdorf.
Dea wore only one blouse from silvery thread as mini-dress, silvery lady-shoes with high heels, a black jacket as fur-imitation and a silvery handbag.
The snow was about twenty-five centimeters high and the temperature lay about ten degrees under zero. Nevertheless she had taken the bus and the subway.
In this evening, Dea won the first price, a silver-plated goblet. At the competition she had imitated the dance of John Travolta.
Not only the men, but also the women had applauded Dea Aphrodite continuously.

At the beginning of year 1978, anuses some written and telephonic correspondence between Walter and the bread-ago Angelo, the two decide on that finish February they themselves meets in Milan.
They wanted to live together, as soon as in about four years Walter's civilian service was finished in the outside service in the foreign countries.

Of course, that already over eighteen-year old brother Mimmo stood
freely to decide, whether he wanted to live together or not.
The sister Elena already had a provider, but she had always to find a
place of refuge for herself and her children at the brothers.
She was married with the ten year older Giovanni Dossola. The two had
an about six months old son Roberto and the future son Andrea was on
the way.

The suitcase for the trip to Milan was already packed also with an
evening dress and other lady's accessories. Walter as woman wanted to
surprise Angelo at his birthday-party.
For the vacation was already applied and approves, as in the company
simultaneously several workers became sick.
The employer had placed him in front of the election, to postpone the
vacations about ten days or to be quit. Walter remained nothing other
than to postpone the trip.

In the night from the Thursday to the Friday, the third March, Walter was
invaded by a startling vision.

**He saw in the vision, Angelo drives a Fiat Mini in the Milanese
streets and the passenger was Walter.
Angelo wanted to prevent, that Walter went back to Berlin. That's
why he provoked an accident.
At this accident Walter should injure himself so, that he must sit in
the wheelchair for life, all the, to be depended on the help of
Angelo, but Walter died at this accident.**

On Saturdays-evening Walter received at telegram from Elena with the
unpleasant message, that on the third March of the year 1978 Angelo
died at a deadly motorcycle-accident, exactly thirteen days before his
twenty-third birthday.

Walter would have departed at the most dearly immediately, but he
required a vacation-residence approval for Italy, because of the service-
issue and the Italian consulate was closed until Monday.
Trips without authorization for Walter was too risky.
He had to would make the service additional in the case, that he would
be caught and that would have ruined all future-plans.
On Monday, he could take care of everything for the trip and said
information also in the company that he must to Italy because of a
fatality.

In Milan arrived, he didn't know where he should go, that no one of the relationship was telephonic to reach.

Walter didn't remain other than to go to the boarding school in the Torrazza-Street 80, in the Gallaratesse quarter, where since some years Mimmo has lived.

Walter didn't believe his eyes. He knew that the boarding school deceives the state, for years.

At that time, as he had applied the passport, he experienced that the boarding school still collected money for board and lodging, although Walter lived already for years in Berlin.

Walter saw one of the boarding school-founders, the somewhat corpulent man that have difficulty in walking, that tolerates and even promotes the young-prostitution and drug spreading.

Walter heard from this man that Mimmo and the relationship were just by Angelo's burial and that on the day after it him will pick up. So Walter slept in Mimmo's bed.

On the day after it, uncle Vittorio, Mimmo and unfortunately also Agnese came. Walter didn't know, where he should live, that was no longer possible be quartered with Angelo.

Hypocritically, Agnese offered herself, to receive Walter in the time, that he was in Milan. Meanwhile she had an old two-room-apartment in the Panigarola-Street 8.

Walter had very big misgivings at Agnese to live. He knew quite exactly as the end became, but according the circumstances, didn't remain him other than to assume. Mimmo promised also to be there and to sleep, in the middle of the double bed between Walter and Agnese.

After already three days, Agnese provoked a dispute with Walter in the presence of Mimmo.

She made him the reproach, that through his birth to have destroyed her life.

With black humor, Walter apologized at all been born to be and made clear Agnese, that about nine months before his birth not he himself with Domenico had had a good time sexually, but she.

In the days after it, the atmosphere sharpened itself so strongly to, that Walter decided, as fast as possibly to depart.

During a conversation with Mimmo, that the whole squabbling had been get of, Walter said to him, that he wanted to visit Angelo again and then back to Berlin wanted to go, that he could no longer endure Agnese's nastiness.

Mimmo told Walter, what on the day, as Angelo died, were happened. At this time, he couldn't make head or tail of it, but now it made a sense.

Mimmo reported:

► In the morning of the same day, that Angelo died, Angelo came to visit us. He was been in a very cheerful mood and told, that in a short time Walter will arrive in Milan, and they common wanted to do the preparations for a common apartment, so that Walter could soon definite back to Italy.
Agnese received panic, as she that heard and a vehement dispute erupted between her and Angelo.
Angelo did clear Agnese, that it was already decided matter, whether she wanted or not.
Still before Angelo went away, Agnese had forced him absolute to drink lemonade. Shortly after it, Angelo felt unwell.
Hours later came the message that Angelo died through a heavy motorcycle-accident.
Mimmo could also not understand, why Agnese insisted on it, that her naturally son Angelo becomes a postmortem, and although she knew, that Angelo had wanted to have a cremation, she had refused to fill, the last wish of the dead. ◄

During the last visit on the cemetery the district Baggio, Walter believed to hear the voice of Angelo out of the grave that him said, that he should to start everything for the realization as woman that he himself no longer can allow to wait.

Before the return trip to Berlin Walter quietly spoke with Elena. She told him under other, that she didn't want to have the inheritance of Domenico and asked, whether he wanted to have her share.
Walter, that suspected a later dispute, refused thanking, and proposed, possible to give it at Mimmo.

1977 – Angelo & nephew Roberto

The inheritance, that Domenico has left (1978-1979)

Going back to Berlin, Walter hoped to receive soon, his share of the inheritance, the Domenico him had left. With this he wanted to start everything to the realization to woman.

True Walter wanted to have himself operated in Italy, there ace born Italian he would have had few of problem, but anuses the death of Angelo, Agnese had closed him all ways.

Domenico had left a savings book with an amount of eleven-thousand German marks at the post office Hamburg, and shortly before his death he had bought some properties in Sicily, to it came other properties, that been given him from him uncles from America.
Domenico had decree in his legacy, that his descendants Walter, Elena, Angelo and Mimmo should receive the inheritance, and Mrs. Marianne Margarete Hohenstein born Noth a life-long usufruct.

On the basis of Italian right the testator's children Walter, Elena, Angelo and Mimmo are entitled everyone one fourth of the total-estate.
Mrs. Hohenstein stands a life-long usufruct at three quarters of the total-estate, in the case of the death the wife of the testator at the total-estate to.
She is relieved from the inventory–and deposit-duty.
The wife of the testator, Agnese Turiano born Fioraso is entitled a life-long usufruct at one quarter of the total-estate.

On eighth October of the year 1977, at the district court of Milan, although Agnese knew that Domenico had left a will, she made following **wrong** statement:
▶ On the 17 August 1977, died my husband Turiano Domenico born in S. Teresa Riva the **17**-02-1927 resident in S. Teresa Riva province of Messina with domicile in Germany (Berlin) **without to leave a will.**
Therefore he had left as only heirs the signing wife and the children:
Turiano Walter born at the **19**-05-1952, **resident in Arese province of Milan.**
Turiano Elena born in Meledo from Sarego the **26**-09-1953, resident in Castellaro Guidobono province of Alessandria.
Turiano Angelo born in Milan the 16-03-1955, resident in Milan in the Rizzardi-Street 31.
Turiano Mimmo born in Milan the 16-08-1959, resident in Milan in the Torrazza-Street 80.

It gives no other heirs.
The Mr. Turiano Domenico is dead in Taormina.
(Signature from: Fioraso Agnese)
(Signature of court-writer: S. Barons) ◄

One day, Walter received a letter from an alleged *"lawyer"*, Mr.
Moschella from the proximity of Messina in Sicily.
He was the son of the senior lawyer Moschella, that in the 60er years his
lawyer-chamber had in the Corso-Buenos-Aires in Milan.
The senior lawyer Moschella was it, that in the end the 60er years, the
one tried to interrogate Walter over the secret from "Mussolini's
treasure", and he was also entangled in the many illegal matter.
Agnese engaged the alleged lawyer, the Junior Moschella, in order to
persuade respectively to force Walter to renounce on his inheritance-
share in favor of from Agnese.
Walter, although already with a leg in the grave, just he had survived
again an attempted suicide.
He was not ready to renounce on his inheritance-share and already not
at all in favor of from Agnese.
Walter gave a special power of attorney, that the Junior Moschella
authorized, all his share at the properties to auction. The highest bidder
should receive the purchase-contract.

The more problematic transit-way as well as way back to female (1979-1987)

After the last survived attempted suicide in the year 1978 Walter realized, that so he could not continue. Therefore he went completely depressed to his family doctor Dr. med. Hans-Jürgen Kohs in order to seek help and advice.
Dr. Kohs recognized the problem. Therefore he referred him to the gynecologist professor Nevinny-Stickl to the hormone determining and further-treatment in the women-university-hospital in Berlin-Charlottenburg.

The hormone determining produced evidence, that in the area of the laboratory-results one almost hundred percent male determining however was missing the determining the female estrogens.
Professor Nevinny-Stickl was of the opinion, that a person, who has such laboratory-results, itself impossible as woman could feel. Therefore, in principle he refused a hormone-treatment.

This hormone determining is actually the proof, that in the past a manipulation with male hormones with Walter had taken place.
In the year 1959, as he was seven years old, Agnese had induced, that every day, a whole month long, he really was raped with male hormone-injections.

After the refusal of professor Nevinny-Stickl, Walter fell into the acute depression again.
The neighbor Lieselotte persuaded him to go, after a renewed suicide-attempt, for the first time in the psychiatric clinic in Berlin-Spandau in the year 1979.
In the psychiatric clinic a young-woman psychologist immediately recognized the problem. She declared Walter that he is not crazy, but only he is captured in the untrue body.
The young-woman psychologist promised Walter to clarify professor Nevinny-Stickl about the problem.

Anuses this of clearing professor Nevinny-Stickl prepared to carry out the hormone-treatment, but only after the vacation in about six to eight weeks. Meanwhile he should begin the psychotherapy at Mr. Dr. Haupt in the women-university-hospital in Berlin-Charlottenburg.

After about two months, before beginning of the treatment, professor
Nevinny-Stickl did a new hormone determining.
Professor Nevinny-Stickl was surprised, that the hormone-results had
changed. The male had sunk and the female climbed, also Walter's look
was unequivocally more female.
Professor Nevinny-Stickl asked Walter, if he himself hormone-
preparations would have procured elsewhere, but Walter assured, that
that was not the case.

In May 1979, Walter could begin the psychotherapy with Dr. Haupt. First
Dr. Haupt was skeptical, but in running of the treatment he became ever
more confident from the femininity of Walter, that since some time he
could push through to be spoken to as Rosa.
Dr. Haupt was also confident, that the nightmares, the Rosa since her
birth haunt and torment, consequences and memories were from
startling experiences, that she had experienced with the birth and the
first seven years of her life.
Dr. Haupt was also of the opinion, that the sexual relationship between
Rosa and her uncle Vittorio, in August of the year 1959, provoked not
from Rosa had become, but from the children-abuser uncle Vittorio. After
all Vittorio was twenty-three and Rosa sieves year old.
In secret, Rosa had fallen in love in Dr. Haupt, but unfortunately it turned
into nothing.
In the year 1980, during the nerves-medicals assessments now is
spoken continually from trans-sexuality, what at least the hermaphrodite-
status respectively the neutral position between both sexes respected.
Takes place the ridge applications at the health insurance company to
the support of sex-changing operations.

The Confidence-Medical-Service of Berlin-West, by the order of the
health insurance company, it had placed itself against Rosa from the
beginning on, although all medical and nerves-medicals examinations
were in favor of Rosa.
One of the trust-doctors had claimed even cold bloody opposite Rosa,
that at her a sex-conversion not worthwhile will be, that anyway she
would have to live only a few until highest ten years.

**Why the Confidence-Medical-Service of Berlin-West had really
sabotaged Rosa?**
*In the same year in Berlin-West, as Rosa had put the propositions,
further nine German citizens had applied the sex-conversion,
among them was also one the later known become as Romy
Haag (*).*
Rosa was the single foreigner and she was refused as single.

Was the reason, because she was Italian, or because she is a hospital-experiment from the fifties years?

(*) Romy Haag (* 1. January 1951 in Scheveningen, Netherlands – Romy Haag was born under the names **Edouard Frans Verbaarsschott**).
She is a German dancer, singer, former nightclub-proprietress and one of the most famous trans-sexual wives Germany.

After refusals from the health insurance company for the expenses-takeover for a surgical neologism the nose in the year 1979, that outsized and hooked nose was (one typical witch-nose), and in the year 1980 over the expenses-takeover for a sex-changing breast-operation. Under incriminating conditions Rosa had to work for the money, and after these refusals, even the operations in order to give.
The operations took place at Mrs. Dr. Flemming, not as agreed in the clinic Berlin-Steglitz, but in her private-practice.
Later, one would determine, that Mrs. Dr. Flemming a bungler is and both operations from her were bungled. Several operations were necessary, in order to repair the damage.

In July 1979, Rosa had to would quit at the company wool-manufacture Lorenit, that she could do no heavy work, and that the company refused to give her an easy work.
After a medical examination, by the order of the employment office because of a retraining, one determined that is existing heavy wear-appearances the spinal column with posture-defects. Therefore, one recommended only one activity with alternate runs, seats and standing, for example boss-secretary.
The retraining should begin after acquisition of the secondary modern school's diploma.
After about five months of unemployment Rosa began, against the advice of the employment office, as kitchen-help at the restaurant Waldbaude in the Bernauer-Street 139 in Berlin-Tegel. The possessors of the restaurant K. Ebbecke had the bad habit all meal-rests, that came back to use for the other guests again.
End of June 1980, Rosa was quit, as she was sick. After legal proceedings she received spoken compensation.

One day, Rosa received a telephone call of Agnese. She tried again to persuade Rosa to renounce on the Domenico's inheritance.
Rosa made unequivocally clear, that she would never renounce.
At the same time, Rosa had also communicated her, that she will have herself operated soon. Although Rosa had not said, about which

operation it was, Agnese had screamed horribly: ***"No!!! What should the people think?"***
Rosa finished the telephone call without to say goodbye.

Some time late, Rosa received a letter from the alleged lawyer Moschella junior, with the offer:
▶ Rosa should receive the entire savings-book-amount with the eleven thousand German marks that Domenico had left at the post office Hamburg. Ace services in return, Rosa should renounce on her shares at the properties. ◀
Rosa knew, that with it she had a very big loss, but she had no alternative *(it is better to have one sparrow in the hand, as a pigeon on the roof)*. That's why she was agreeing with it, but after it she saw no money and for many years she has also nothing more heard from the lawyer.

One day, to that time, as Rosa herself still exaggerated made-up how a paradise-bird, she heard when leaving the house where she lived, a woman about fifty years old to her husband whispers, that she is probably a whore.
Rosa, completely indifferent and with the nose upward, turned around and said to the woman: ***"So what? Because you are not in the situation to masturbate your husband sexually, he must get himself with me the satisfaction!"***
The woman turned around to her husband and she giving him angrily a slap in the face, although Rosa knew no one from both.

Rosa received two clinic-addresses from professor Nevinny-Stickl, where the sex-changing operation could take place, why in the women-university-hospital in Berlin-Charlottenburg was not possible.
Rosa sent the propositions per certified letter to the both clinics, a clinic in Kiel and the other in Munich.

Rosa
alias Dea APHRODITE

Mai 1980

Since the health insurance company refused also the expenses-takeover
for the sex-changing operations, Rosa remained nothing other, as the
legal costs insurance with the German labor union in Berlin-West in claim
to take.
Unfortunately Rosa had noticed too late, that the labor union represents
not only the work force but also the employers and the health insurance
company.
With the ridge legally proceedings began therefore a really legal-war
against the health insurance company, that itself on recommendation of
the Confidence-Medical-Service, the health insurance company denied
to acknowledge Rosa's rights.

Rosa received answer only of the clinic Großhadern of the university
Munich. Professor Dr. W. Eicher asked Rosa to a before-conversation
and to the medical examination because of the sex-changing operations.
During the before-conversation and medical examination, professor Dr.
W. Eicher had no doubts at the urgent necessity of the operations.
Therefore he asked Rosa herself to report again to the purpose an
operation-date, as soon as the expenses-takeover of the health
insurance company was available.
Mysterious-way the health insurance company approved in a flash the
expenses for the operation, without to wait for a judgment. The lawyer
suspected in order to prevent a precedent, but Rosa experienced the
true reason month after it.
End of December 1980, it was finally so wide. Professor Dr. W. Eicher
operated Rosa. Two weeks after it, a correction was necessary that not
equally possibly was to do with the first operations.
The health insurance company wanted the expenses for the correction
first doesn't pay, because it was of the opinion, that that same with the
first operation had been able to do.
The court demanded from professor Dr. W. Eicher the medical
documents of Rosa. So Rosa had experienced why the health insurance
company approved in a flash the expenses for sex-changing operations.
In accordance with the medical documents: During the before-
conversation and medical examination professor Dr. W. Eicher had
determined irregularities with Rosa. The male sex-organ had cancer and
she had probably not long to live, if she not quickly operated would
become.

Start 1981 in Germany, the law for the official register of that of first
name–and sex-alteration was already passed, but in Italy this law was
not yet decided and it was not to be foreseen when this would be the
case. That's why Rosa had to apply for that in Germany.

Unfortunately Rosa had no other alternative, as first to apply for the German naturalization and consequently the loss of the Italian citizenship.
In order to lose no time, the naturalization and entry-alteration of the first name-and sex was processed simultaneous.
Rosa adjudicated to apply for herself the first name Evelyn, in order to avoid confusion, with the nearly same age cousin Rosa from America, who has also the same surname.

At twenty-first April 1981, Rosa received handed over the German naturalization-document (records-number: I E 53 - 113 789) from the Senator for Interior in Berlin-West.
With decision of the district court Berlin-Schöneberg of the fourth June 1981 is decided (records-number: 70 III 160/81), that the petitioner is that the petitioner is affiliated to look at as the female sex and henceforth the first name Evelyn leads.

Short time late, Evelyn applied at the first registry office in Berlin-West the entry in the Berlin's birth-book. That was possible on the basis of a law for special cases.
After the woman-registrar had ordered a copy the entry in the birth-book from the registry office of Milan, on the twenty-fifth January 1982 she was written down in the Berlin's birth-book (number: 189/1982).
Evelyn received a copy of the birth-entry of the Milanese registry office. So she received the proof, that by the birth she bore the surnames Froletti and immediately she was to get rid of the orphanage, although that Agnese had always denied and claimed her maniac is.

The damages that Agnese had caused by Evelyn's birth and the first eight years in her life they are almost no longer to repair. The male hormone-delivery that Agnese by Evelyn had induced as she sieve year old was, had to the consequence that she had received already with eight years her voice was breaking, she was strong physical hirsute, spinal-column-problems and other physical afflictions.

Evelyn
alias
Dea APHRODITE

11. Juni 1981

The female hormone-therapy that Evelyn received since 1979, it could also not to repair the hairy-problem.
After long unemployment Evelyn was written sick two years because of her physical and mental afflictions.
A cure-proposition was put in year 1983. It was refused because of face-disfigurement through beard; against the will of Evelyn, a pension was approved for it because of unemployable-ness, first for two years then rearranged permanently.
Evelyn was herself forced to muffled-up, if she left the apartment.

An electric depilatory-treatment was begun for the face, but quickly it had to broken off because the health insurance company wanted to pay only one fraction and Evelyn had no money about it to pay.
Also it became many other therapy-treatments to elimination applied the face-hairy-problem, but without success.
With it in year 198, the cosmetic surgeon Dr. Detlef Witzel had, as first operates a small test with success by Evelyn; but after it, he itself doesn't trust to operate further, although he had promised it.

At this time Evelyn is completely be at an end, not only bodily, but especially also mental. The nightmares have come back heavily; worst it is however the permanent war with the health insurance company.
In September 1981, she will deliver at the second time into the nerves-clinic Spandau for about six weeks because of suicide-attempt.
Four weeks later, Evelyn is received again for about four weeks on the basis of a suicide-attempt. She drank one glassful with twenty more percent "H2 O2" solution (Hydrogen-super-oxide-solution).
Four days later, she is delivered again for about two weeks because of a suicide-attempt, after she had tried to cut open the arteries at both wrists.

In the autumn 1981, Evelyn did acquaintance with Peter Frenz. He was a few years older and much shorter than she.
Peter was many too nicely and helpful. Although Evelyn had no good feeling, in the Christmas Eve the two gets engaged, as she was in the nerves-clinic Spandau.
Peter persuaded Evelyn, that she gave him a big and valuable collection from memorial-coins as engagement-gift.
Unfortunately, Evelyn became a slave to him. She perceived much too late that she was fall on a marriage-fraud.
After about seven years, definite she could break away from him. Evelyn reported Peter on the basis of marriage-frauds and hand over of the memorial-coins-collection.
Peter had alleged the numismatic collection no longer and he was not either in the position to compensate them. Therefore, the judge

condemned him at Evelyn, to pay twenty German marks per month up to
ten years long. Evelyn was of the opinion, that he was not punished
sufficiently. Therefore she cursed him with cancer.
A few years later, Peter died after long sorrow agonizingly at larynx-
cancer.

An evening in the year 1982 (or 1983?), as again Evelyn found no way
out from her predicament, she took a whole packet powerful sleeping
pills in the hope, never to wake up again.
The pills instead of to give Evelyn in deep sleep, it had reached only the
total opposite.
About midnight, Evelyn was dressed with only shoes, false fur-jacket,
handbag with a hammer and otherwise nothing; she ordered herself a
taxi, and she went to the Berlin Savings Bank (Berliner Sparkasse) in the
old part of town Spandau.
There she stark naked, she opened with the check card the first bank-
door and with the hammer she smashed the pane of the second door;
then she made herself comfortable at the bank-director's desk and
waited on the police.
After a while, the police-command came and brought Evelyn at the
police-presidency. As the police officials become conscious, that she
didn't want to rob the bank, but that only one help-scream was, about on
her predicament to do attention, she was freed again and the issue
hushed up.
The Berlin Newspaper broke following headline: **"Naked woman with
beard broke with a sledge-hammer into the Berlin Savings Bank in
the old part of town Spandau"**.

In the year 1985, treatment in the Clinic Westend and carrying out a
second face-operation.
Here was surgically distanced the whiskers and the Adam's apple
demolished in the area of the larynx.
Unfortunately after several months the whiskers came back in the fuller
starch.
Several years later, Evelyn had no other alternative, as in the clinical
complex in Berlin-Moabit, as guinea pig several x-ray-irradiations in the
area of the whiskers over herself to let go out.
This treatment with x-rays had let vanish the whiskers only for about a
half year, then they came back exactly so strong how before; and
because of the higher risk, no doctor as well as surgeon wanted more
her to treat as well as to operate in the face-area.

Evelyn
alias
Dea APRODITE

März 1982

Evelyn
alias
Dea APRODITE

September 1982

Since the first breast-operations in the year 1980, that of Mrs. Dr. Flemming was bungled, were several treatments and altogether five or six breast-operations had become necessary and many years of legal proceedings against the health insurance because of the expenses-takeover, in order to repair the damage.
Not until the last operation in the year 1997 had been successful. Since then she has no troubles more in the breasts.

On the first August 1987, in a judicial expert opinion (records-number: S 72 Kr 404/86), professor Dr. med. D. Kadach wrote among other things following report:

▶ **Conducts from the health insurance company with propositions of sex-changing operations since 1978:**
1. Since 5/1979 the hormone-medications were from the health insurance company been paid, the hormone-medications were necessary to enforce the ford-ago feminine determining, after from two neurological departments as secured was looked at, that this trans-sexuality about one with female determining is it. … It was fixed, that with 2-year constant claim under the psychotherapy from medical side then by all operations should be consented that also in the area the outer appearance to contribute to the female determining.
2. The proposition to the first breast-operation taken place end of 1979 - Start 1980. The health insurance company refused it. The patient believes, with it a second argument of the foreigner-hostility by the health insurance company, to have noticed. After the refusal, the patient describes her feeling with following words: "I wanted the further theater with processes to keep out of the way, therefore I took the trouble to show my good will, and a share at these operations I myself wanted to take on." The operation in year 1980 therefore took place at Mrs. Dr. Flemming on own sharing of costs.
3. The conservative x-ray-irradiation in the hospital Spandau Lynar-Street because of stronger scar-formation in the area of the breasts is made to charges of the health insurance company.
4. 1981, the stationary treatment took place in the Forest-Hospital (Waldkrankenhaus) to operative breasts-capsule-blowing up and scar-correction be made to charges of the health insurance company. Here exists however the suspicion, that with inaccurate admission-diagnosis the health insurance company was not taught timely about the actual event.
5. On the occasion of the first sex-changing operation in the area of the abdomen in the clinical complex Großhadern in Munich as well be made the proposition-position by the health insurance company.

The expenses-takeover was first refused, then however in the contradiction-procedure approves.

6. The operative treatments of the chin-beard and upper-lip-beard as well as the distance a big Adam's apple as well be made to apply by the health insurance company and from the health insurance company approves. As a result of the principles of the health insurance company this only under economically justifiable point of view to approve, in each case critical treatment-expenses were been chosen. Under these points of view is until 1985 the whiskers-operations approves and been paid.

<u>Final remark:</u>

It is with the now 35-year old patient most important if about a trans-sexuality with female determining.

This means, that the genetic factor neither ace cub quietly ace girl fully distinctive was, …

This determining led to most heavily nerve complications up to the years 1982/1983. She improved herself, because since 1978 a treatment the psychosomatic problems of the trans-sexuality started and the patient the feeling gave, that she can live on her role as woman.

Of neurologists' site will confirm the sex of this person as woman.

… This represents an illness as well as an illness-similar-condition in the sense of the Federal-insurance-routine.

… Under these points of view, it is incomprehensible, why the health insurance company has refused the first operation in the area of the breast. It has remained without doubts that the patient has already applied for this first operation as well as their expenses-takeover by the health insurance company.

… It should therefore be medically indisputable; that the health insurance company would have already this first operation must pay.

… All these consequences however the health insurance company also has with to be responsible, that first she each help with the first-operation refused. This was duty-adverse.

… Also that is inexplicable, that the health insurance company itself at the latest since the establishing of the female determining the diseased body-condition over the treatment-duty of all operations in the area of the outer body-form as well as also necessary medicines-treatment in the clear had to be.

The establishing of the female determining took place 1979/1980 from recognized clinics and university-departments, so that there could be only few doubts over it. The health insurance company therefore even has through incomprehensible stand to these medical questions to continuing complications by the patient contributed.

Annoy and expenditure with the proposition-position through the patient in the interest of the nerve condition been able to become avoid, if the

health insurance company itself of an expert doctor or expert would have assured, that above all the trans-sexual problem would have recognized in time.
The health insurance company was therefore called for the treatment-duty already that of the first breast-operation. She has refused this however, what has contributed to further health-disturbances.
She is cost-reimbursable also to all further sex-changing operations. ... (Professor Dr. med. D. Kadach) ◄

Dea APHRODITE-KALI, the amalgamation of two goddesses (1987-1994)

Evelyn would really be sabotaged from that "families", health insurance company, authorities and so on and were put obstacles her in the way. Even the mayor Werner Salomon (1979 —1992 mayors of Spandau, Berlin), although Evelyn had several dates with him in the citizen-office's consulting hours, he had each time denied.
In the year 1985, the mayor Werner Salomon even said in the presence of witnesses, when Evelyn met him during he was leaving the town hall, word-for-word: ***"With such a person I want to have not to do!"***

It something in this Time, that Dea Aphrodite's soul had merged itself with the soul of the goddess fertilizer to at double-goddess, therefore the cruelty the mankind to endure and to survive. So Evelyn turned into Dea APHRODITE-KALI, "the goddess of the love and the cruelty". After all, all medals have two sides, "the kindliness and the nastiness"; one cannot exist without the other.

End of the year 1986, Evelyn did a renewed advances at her "families". Hypocritically, Agnese offered itself, that meanwhile she had bought a three-room-apartment in the Verga-Street 20 in Mombretto of Mediglia province of Milan, to receive Evelyn to itself. Ridge in the vacation, then for always she should come back to Italy.
In January, Evelyn went with the cat Mischita to the apartment of Agnese and the brother Mimmo; Mischita should remain in Italy till also Evelyn for always there would remain.
Although Evelyn since the burial of bread-ago Angelo in March 1978 had been no longer in Italy and the building, where Agnese had bought the apartment, it something built finished since some months, Evelyn already knew it.

She was already there a few days before the departures, in fact with her astral body.
Interesting is, that she cannot do such mystic trips on order, but only in true emergencies.

Agnese complained, that she had lost quantity money through the bought shares, that she had to sell again with big loss after short time, in order to buy the apartment.

Agnese confessed also, that she had induced, at the bank in the presence and consent from Elena, that the shares had deposited, that in the case of her own death *"only"* the daughter Elena should inherit. Agnese confirmed with this confession, that her own descendant was only *"a means to an end"*.
Well yes, Evelyn was for Agnese already at that time *"only"* leverage. That been born Evelyn as hermaphrodite, an experiment-breakdown was. Therefore, after inducement of Agnese, Evelyn was changed to the boy, because Agnese could reach only so, that Domenico married her. Mimmo, that is exactly the image of his father Domenico, was *"only"* a life- and age-safeguarding; that she could tyrannize and terrorize him exactly as her then husband Domenico.

Beginning the year 1987, Evelyn wanted at her ex-colleagues, friends, relationship and the family Ratano for the first time introduces itself as woman and therefore they all shock.
Evelyn was surprised very much, the family Ratano, that she looked at as own family, the friends and ex-colleagues at the company "LA. ME. PRE." had received her with joy and they all were not surprised to see Evelyn as woman, in the opposite, they all had suspected and had known, that it was only one question of the time.
Even a same age ex-colleague, that unfortunately meanwhile already was married, said to Evelyn, because in November 1969 she was missing from Milan, he had had to marry another woman.
In opposite, even Elena, that had probably been instigated by Agnese, and her two sons Roberto and Andrea had withheld, that they have an aunt, that earlier an uncle was, they tried not to remark to let, that them the issue didn't fit. Evelyn had felt that unequivocally, although she had not left it remark itself.
The remaining relationship tried to find excuses; about at all not to have to see Evelyn, at least Evelyn had felt it so.

At the occasion, as Evelyn was in Milan, she engaged the lawyer Attilia Fracchia; in the Visconti-of-Modrone-Street number 32, about also in Italy to obtain the acknowledgment of the name- and sex-alteration.
With date of the twentieth January 1989, the court of justice of Milan acknowledged the name- and sex-alteration (records-number: 2983/88 R. G.) and then ordered registry office of Milan to write down the note of the judgment in the original births-book.
At the police-presidency of the Milan, Evelyn put also the proposition on residence permit (registration's number: 205026), that first for one year valid was, then it was extended until December 1988.

Evelyn
alias
Dea APHRODITE-KALI

Januar 1987

January 1987

Evelyn
alias
Dea APHRODITE-KALI

03. September 1988

Evelyn had the eleven thousand German mark, that had left Domenico and that she should receives as service in return for her shares at the properties, intellectual she already had view it as loss, as she was spoken to in April 1987 of Agnese, that wanted to have a special-authority for the properties.
Evelyn got Agnese ready, that she because of the agreement a special-authority only will sign after receipt of the eleven thousand German mark. The twenty-sixth April, at the notary Pasquale Iannello in Milan, had Mimmo and Agnese in own person and as representatives of Elena; a special-authority signed, the Evelyn authorizes to receive the eleven thousand German mark. After disposal of the formalities with Mrs. Marianne Margarete Hohenstein born Noth, that in the property of the Post Office savings book was, Evelyn could collect the money.
The fifth January 1988, Evelyn signed a special-authority at the notary Pasquale Iannello that Agnese authorized the properties to sell in Santa Teresa of Riva province of Messina.
Some months later, Evelyn received a letter from the alleged lawyer, the Junior Moschella, in order of Agnese, although that for Evelyn the issue had locked with very big loss.
The alleged lawyer wanted, that Evelyn transfers him the eleven thousand German mark, he would have her after it supposedly transferred back.
Evelyn made clear to him that she is not stupid and furthermore through the remittance first to Italy and then back to Germany a strong exchange rate-loss would have.

On the third September 1988, as Evelyn was at a visit in Milan, she went with Mimmo and Agnese to a musical festival of Riccardo Fogli (* 21. Octobers 1947 in Pontedera Italy, he is an Italian singer. From 1966 to 1973, he sang in the group Pooh. Then, he left the group for his solo career. Riccardo Fogli won the San-Remo-Festival 1982 with the title "Storie Di Tutti I Giorni").

Riccardo Fogli asked Evelyn, as she asked him for an autograph, whether she wanted to go with him in his dressing room, but the shyly Evelyn has not dared, although Mimmo had recommend her.

One day, Evelyn Agnese requested her to explain, why she had by the birth the surname Froletti and why she was pushed into an orphanage. Agnese responded completely aggressively and claimed, although Evelyn had submitted the photocopy of the original-birth certificate, that she is a liar and maniacs and that the document is a forgery.
A few days later, Evelyn took the cat Mischita and went back to Berlin.

She broke off the contact with Agnese, only with Mimmo, there was still written correspondence.

As Evelyn after the stay in Milan in September 1988 went back to Berlin, Agnese had started ready again to make Evelyn with the relationship badly, and so a return to Italy to do impossibly.
However, shortly after it Evelyn received a letter from Elena, that her told (without statements of reasons), that she shut nothing more with her wanted to have, and that *"she should remain, where the pepper grows!"*
Evelyn answered, if that her wish is, and then she exists for her even also no longer.
Since at that time, there was between Evelyn and Elena for about twenty years of silence.

In the year 1990, Evelyn had invited Mimmo, to spend a few months in the summer-vacations in Berlin.
Mimmo came in July, but unfortunately not alone, Agnese had simply gone too, although she was not invited and had not asked either, whether she should come along.
Evelyn did "grin and bear it" and has nevertheless received her. Although Agnese for the whole stay no single pfennig had paid, she always had what to nag and tried to provoke dispute constantly.
After the birthday of Mimmo on the sixteenth August, Evelyn had then thrown out Agnese with all her suitcases.

On the day after it, one of the Italian consulates came in company of two police. He reported, that Agnese had claimed, that Evelyn had thrown out her on the street without money.
Evelyn and Mimmo explained the man from the Italian consulate and the police, that Agnese no right would have, furthermore Mimmo confirmed, that she would have three million Italian lire in the handbag. Mimmo still remained for about six weeks in Berlin.
Some months late, Evelyn received mail of the court; Agnese demanded from Evelyn maintenance, that she would not have supposedly sufficiently. Evelyn explained the court, first that Agnese of no right would have, secondly that she receives two pensions and an owner-occupied flat would have, against that Evelyn would only have a small pension and must as well live to the rent.

Riccardo Fogli
und Autogramm

03. September 1988

Riccardo Fogli and autograph

In the year 1991, as it went for Evelyn no longer further and again she no hope more saw, she decided herself with help that "white magic" to have prepared a particular double-sided amulet.

She studied the three-volumes book "practice magic", that she had bought by her last visit in Milan, and decided for a double-sided locket from three-fourths gold and a fourth copper, that she could not carry pure copper because of an allergy.

Exactly at her thirty-nine birthdays she bought the corresponding material and gave the order by a jeweler, to have prepared a double-sided locket.

The locket should be engraved the first talisman of the Venus on the skin-side.

► The first talisman of the Venus serves, to control the spirits of the planet.

It promotes grace and honors and one can, with his help, each art practices, that under the reign of the planet fall.

Indoors around at the edge is incised the names of the angels: Nogahiel, Acheliah, Socohia und Nangariel. ◄

The first talisman of the Jupiter should be engraved on the view-side of the locket.

► The first talisman of the Jupiter represents a certain interest, and it became, as also certified, from him of a historical personality application done.

It carries the inscription (how usually between two circles): «Gloria and wealth into the house of him; and his justice lasts eternally», from the psalm CXII, 3.

This talisman, drawn on parchment, one put on again on the body of the Count Anselm, bishop of Würzburg, in the night of the ninth February 1749.

One therefore says, that it was the big power of the talisman, that him allowed, to reach his high position, and to earn riches and power himself, what has helped him, to escape the attacks of his many enemies.

The same talisman serves also, to discover the hidden treasures, and to protect the celebrating against the evil spirits during the rite of the Jupiter. ◄

In the middle from the locket was bordered a small aquamarine, and round about the edge around the personal data of Evelyn were engraved.

On the basis of his, that the particular double-sided amulet is not from pure copper, it could not develop the full magic strength, but too least it went for Evelyn uphill and she was protected by negative strengths.

Since August 1985, Evelyn was represented by the Federal-Association (later renamed in Socially-Association Germany), in the right-dispute against the health insurance company.
The Federal-Association had reached in the year 1988 through court proceeding, that been condemned the health insurance company, to take on the expenses for the operation to again-preparation of the breasts, and in the year 1994 to have to adopt the expenses, for a face-operation through a specialist for plastic surgery.
But unfortunately, because of the encumbrances, no surgeon dared meanwhile to operate more.

Evelyn tried to convince Dr. Detlef Witzel that had meanwhile an own practice in the building of the Hotel Mondial at the Kurfürstendamm 47, to operate her.
Dr. Witzel had refused because he didn't dare; therefore Evelyn would remain not other choice, than to threaten, in the practice to set on fire herself. So after it, those surgeons would have had to operate her, because of the burns.
Under these circumstances the senior consultant Dr. Dr. med. Johannes C. Bruck was recommended, in the Urban-Hospital.
The avaricious Dr. Bruck operated Evelyn in the summer 1994, after the health insurance company had him paid his "privately honorarium" in advance.
Dr. Bruck, that is a capacity in the restoration-surgery, he had out-peeled away almost the whole beard-hair-problem, but he had left strongly suspicious scars. *Whether had slipped him several times the scalpel, or whether he was not quite sober by the operation?*
First, Evelyn had no worries because of the scars, that *by the first consultation's conversation Dr. Bruck had said, that after about two years, a face-lifting is necessary because of the out-peeled of the whiskers, and simultaneous could be corrected with it the old and new scars*.
Unfortunately, Evelyn was so stupid to believe Dr. Bruck, and that herself not to have given in writing.
So three years later, the health insurance company denied taking over the expenses for the correction.
Dr. Bruck had ignored as well as all denies the comment-request of the court, so that Evelyn had lost the process, although her face was already hollow as one empty sack.

At few days anuses the face-operation in the buzzers 1994, Evelyn did the acquaintance with at about twenty-five-year old young one from India, as she was still in the hospital.

Year before the Indian had lost a forearm through a motorcycle-accident.
He had made the court for her, with the argument to want to learn Italian,
in the truth he wanted from Evelyn receive *"French sexual-
instruction"*.
During the engagement Evelyn made clear to him, that she ***didn't*** want
to marry before would be one year past. Although he was about twenty
year younger as she, a beautiful physique had, with his hindrance could
handle well and the sex fantastic and lasting was, she separated from
him.
After about three months she became conscious, that the papers for the
marriage was already applied and also from her same had been signed,
although she wanted to wait least one year.
Wanted the Indian Evelyn to marry, or through manipulation a German
passport?

The second education's way (1994-2005)

August 1994, Evelyn enrolled to the University-Extension-Spandau (VHS Spandau) to the belated acquisition of the main-school-graduation, that because of a wait-list first at the January 1996 she could start. Meantime she attend the courses English as foreign language, basic-level I, II and III.
At the January 1996 she had acquired the main-school-graduation, in June 1997 she received the diploma with following judgments of the performances: mathematics and physics each grade 1 (very good) – English (performance-level II) grade 2 (well) – world-events and chemistry each grade 3 (satisfactory) – and German grade 4 (sufficiently).
At the August 1997 she had acquired the real-school-graduation, in January 1999 she received the diploma with following judgments of the performances: mathematics grade 1 (very good) – physics, chemistry and biology each grade 2 (well) – German, English, History/socially-events, and geography each grade 3 (satisfactory).

Between the main-school-graduation and real-school-graduation Evelyn induced the doctor for neck-noses-ears-medicine, Dr. Sauer at the Kurfürstendamm that of Mrs. Dr. Flemming bungled nose-operation to repair. The health insurance company had tried first the expenses not to take on, but Evelyn had a written explanation from the health insurance company, that had promised, the expenses first to take on, after the elimination of the whiskers was with success enforced.
This written promise, she had had to secure many years before through a woman-lawyer.
Mr. Dr. Sauer had achieved a very good work. He had not only the nose reduces, so that it fitted well to the face-form, but he had also removed the permanent problem with the nosebleed and Evelyn could again breathes quite good.

At the beginning of the year 1999, Evelyn enrolled to the Peter-A.-Silbermann-School in the Blisse-Street 22, to the belated acquisition of the high school graduation, what first end of August could start. In the meantime she attend the courses German ace foreign Language, basic-stone II, in the VHS Spandau, and at the seed Time she tried to renovate her apartment.
She was during the apartment-renovation from the ladder fallen down, so that she had herself badly injured the head and the spinal column.
Through the head-injury, she received again strong memory-

disturbances; nevertheless she began at end of August at the Peter-A.-
Silbermann-School. Unfortunately the leader-accident had left big
memory-disturbances, so that the school-judgment of the performances
in the cellar fell.

After about twenty-three months, on the eighteenth July 2001, Evelyn
received the second certificate with following judgment of the
performances: English and mathematics each grade 4 (sufficiently) –
German, Latin, political world-events and physics each grade 5
(insufficient). Therefore she decided to do at first one year of pause, and
visited in the meantime in the VHS Spandau, the courses German as
foreign language, certificate-grade transition B1/B2, higher level (ZOP
and KDS), German I and II.
On the fifteenth April 2002, she received from that "the European
Language-Certificates" the certificate German with that grade 2 (well).
She had reached a total-result 267,00 of 300,00.
And on the twenty-seventh January 2003, she did also at that "the
European Language-Certificates" the certificate Italian with that grade 1
(very good). She had reached a total-result 270,00 of 300,00, she could
so herself has freed from the drawer Latin.

After recommendation of the headmaster of the Peter-A.-Silbermann-
School, Evelyn changed the school and went to the "Evening-High-
School Prenzlauer Berg" in Berlin-Pankow. There she could begin on the
nineteenth August 2002, but also this change has brought nothing, the
school-performances remained in cellars.
After about twenty-eight months, on the twelfth January 2005, she
received the fifth certificate. The judgment of the performances was
unchanged: political world-events grade 4 (sufficiently) – mathematics
and English each grade 4- (sufficiently) – German grade 5+ (insufficient)
– physics grade 5 (insufficient), so that she would not be admitted to the
high school diploma. Therefore she had decided to do temporary a very
long pause of the school.

Takes parting of Mimmo (2005-2007)

Through the school's stress and other problems, by Evelyn had the stomach-problems strongly exacerbates, so that she confident was, that her time had finally come.
She went in July 2004 to her house-doctor. The married couple Mr. and Mrs. Dr. Kröhn took on the doctor's practice, because Mr. Dr. Kohs had gone in the retirement.
After order a gastro-scope was confirmed a chronically on-smoldering Antrumgastritis (gastritis) with irregular abnormal increase of cells.
Against the will and the knowledge from Evelyn, Mrs. Dr. Kröhn had her prescribed antibiotics, although Evelyn had reported her unequivocally, that she has an antibiotic-allergy.
Evelyn became sicker day by day. After about nine days, she was convinced, that she would not survive the following days, as a physical and mental protection-mechanism entered in force.
The body had refused further antibiotic and foods to take to itself, and she had broken continuously.
Only water she could drink.
After several days she had survived the worst, but not until after more than three months she went her again moderately better. After it, she threatened the practice from Dr. Kröhn with a report of tried murder, if she still afforded herself such error.

Since some time Evelyn felt, that something could not be right. The letters, that she received from Mimmo, seemed so, as if everything in order was, but Evelyn had the feeling more and more, that any or anything shuts not with right things.
After almost twenty years of silence, she wrote to Elena.
Elena had always assured in her letters, that everything was in order and that all are healthy, but the strange feeling of Evelyn became ever stronger.
In the Saturday-afternoon, the sixteenth June 2007, Evelyn received following telegram from Elena: ▶ I am you sorry to have to tell, that our brother Mimmo is put up in the hospital because of a deadly illness.
Urgent, put you with me in contact by telephone.
My telephone number is…
Your sister Elena. ◄

During a telephonic consultation with Elena, Evelyn had experienced, that since a long time Mimmo suffered on intestine-cancer and although he had several operations behind himself, no longer will live long.

Unfortunately no one of the relationship was Evelyn housing ready to offer or to seek; that she herself was sick, and she could herself expensive hotel-expenses doesn't achieve financially. So, everything had moved into the length.

Evelyn questioned the oracle over Mimmo's condition and future, but indifferent which tool she used, whether to put with the mysticism-cards, whether with mysticism-dice, or with mysticism-programs for personnel computers, the answer was always the same.
According to statements of the oracle, Mimmo was dangerously ill and would die soon, but the oracle also said, if Mimmo survived his coming birthday, then, he would have defeated the death and consequently he could live still long.
With this information Evelyn tried to win time.
She promised Mimmo to visit him to his birthday, with the hope, to give live-strength to him.

Meanwhile, end of July, Mimmo was transferred to the "Fondazione Castellini", a nursing- and old people's home in Melegnano province of Milan.
During a telephonic conversation, the woman-doctor, who treated Mimmo, guessed to Evelyn to come soon and told her, that a guest's bed ready has been put for her in the room of Mimmo and that she needs nothing to pay.
Evelyn became conscious, that she must visit Mimmo quickly, otherwise she would lose the possibility to say goodbye to him. Therefore she promised to come within two weeks.
In the night of Wednesday, that eleventh to Thursday, that twelfth July, Evelyn arrived in the "Fondazione Castellini".

Already after very short time, as Evelyn arrived at the "Fondazione Castellini", Mimmo had recovered so well, that the woman-doctor and the nursing-personnel believed in a miracle and a quick convalescence.
Mimmo, who was paralyzed by the abdomen downward, he was downright blooming.
He was cheerfully again and created new energies to the life.
Almost every day, he left drive stroll himself from Evelyn with the wheelchair, received appetite on solid foods and was confident, that he could walk again soon.

Evelyn
alias
Dea APHRODITE-KALI

17. April 2005

Evelyn
alias
Dea APHRODITE-KALI

17. April 2005

After about two weeks, also Evelyn was convinced, that Mimmo will defeat the death, but then unfortunately Agnese had called. She wanted to speak and to meet Evelyn.
Evelyn said, that she wants to think about it, but Agnese had insisted insistent on it, so that Evelyn promised in order to not worry Mimmo unnecessarily.
On the day after it, Evelyn had to pick up Agnese with a taxi and to bring back again, because Agnese claimed that she had no money. Beside the bed and in the presence of Mimmo, Agnese confessed Evelyn, after she had it pretended about fifty-five years long, that the doctors had already determined with the birth, that Evelyn is a hermaphrodite, she also at chronically depressive ill-feeling would suffer, and that she would not live long.
Agnese had also the insolence after that arrogant to be, that she had induced, that the doctors have remove operationally the female organs, because she wanted to have a boy at any price.
Agnese had also admitted, that the so-called vitamin-injects, that she received in the year 1959, no vitamins were, but testosterone-preparations (male sex-hormone preparations).

Agnese was not conscious also after fifty-five years, what she had caused for damage at Evelyn.
After Agnese went back to home, Evelyn could not yet believe, that she had really heard, but Mimmo confirmed her Agnese's confession.

After this day, Mimmo went rapid again more badly, and as Evelyn noticed, that his urine consisted almost only of blood, she became conscious, even if she wanted not yet to have it true, that Mimmo had lost the fight against the death.
The last night, in the delirium, Mimmo had called Evelyn, but not with her first name, but with *"mummy"*.
Saturday, that twenty-eight July 2007, Evelyn becomes clear, that it is only about hours.
She calls Elena and after Agnese and tells them, that he comes to the end. Shortly after it, a neighbor brought Agnese by car.

In the afternoon, that here called woman-doctor took Evelyn aside and explained her, that Mimmo could no longer, and that he wants goes. She should bring Agnese home and comes back quickly with a suit.
Evelyn was to it however emotionally not in the situation, and she didn't want to leave Mimmo in his last hour alone.
Evelyn had called Elena again, but she answered only, that she would come to burial.

The woman-doctor gave to Mimmo an injection and went. After then
Evelyn sat beside him and held the whole time his hand, Agnese sat at
the bed-end.

***Evelyn noticed, that they were not alone in the room, but also many
of the relationship, that already deceased was, also the brother
Angelo and the father Domenico there were. They all kindly showed
Evelyn the symbol of the death, as well as the transformation with
the words, that they all will meet with her.***
***Evelyn became conscious, that she would finally die with sixty-two
years that this symbol will only come in this age again.***

At about sixteen o'clock, Mimmo something very weak, but quietly with
full consciousness, he wanted at sheet of paper and something to
character. Before he had eaten even an ice.
Evelyn gave him a leaf and a ballpoint pen, but he had no strength more.

Evelyn turned around shortly to Agnese and didn't believe her eyes.
Agnese sat clung at the bed-end and fixed Mimmo. She looked like as a
vulture, which could not wait, to rush upon on the corpse.
Evelyn ordered her, that to omit and to leave Mimmo in peace.
About thirty minutes after sixteen o'clock, Mimmo produced no life-signs
more. Evelyn rang after the woman-doctor, but she could confirm only
the death.
Mimmo died exactly nineteen days before his forty-eighth birthday.

Evelyn knew that Mimmo wanted to have a cremation, but she knew
also, that Agnese would not admit that. Therefore she tried it with
cunning.
Evelyn communicated Elena by telephone, that Mimmo is dead and
asked, whether she would know, that he has want a cremation. But
Elena claimed not to have known about it.
Evelyn called the woman-doctor into another room and explained her
Mimmo's last will.
The woman-doctor first tried with cunning, that Agnese would admit it,
then with persuasion, to explain her, that the last will is to be respected,
so that Agnese didn't remain remaining other, than to agree.

Mimmo

02. August 2007

Agnese asked Evelyn, her with the burial- and all other formalities, to be helpful.
Evelyn had agreed but not for Agnese but for Mimmo, with the emphasis, that middle of August she would went back to Berlin.
Thursday, that second August, after the mass for the dead, Mimmo's body was transferred to the crematory in Lambrate a quarter of Milan, where he was cremate on the day after it.

The family met in the bar that "Fondazione Castellini". Shortly after uncle Vittorio was to Evelyn in order to talk with her, from wide she noticed aunt Maria, Vittorio's wife, who they observed very jealously.
Evelyn immediately became clear, that Maria knew about the at that time love-relationship between Evelyn and Vittorio.

Evelyn accompanied and helped Agnese with the burial- and all other formalities. A savings book of Mimmo was quit with about two thousand-five hundred Euro at the consumption-cooperative Coop.
Evelyn wanted to renounce her quarter, but as Elena her share wanted to have, what was her good right, the Coop decided to divide the amount and to send everyone her inheritance per bank-check.
Evelyn had, after redemption of the bank-check, the amount at Agnese transferred. Of course, she had first take off the bank-expenses.
There was a community-bank-account of Agnese and Mimmo with at amount of about ten thousand Euro, although Agnese claimed, that she had no money, and therefore also the relationship for the burial-expenses had begged.
The community-bank-account was dissolved and one new in Mombretto on the name of Agnese furnished, for that of late Evelyn and a neighbor an authority received.
Also the almost new car of Mimmo should be sold, but the time was too short, therefore Agnese had sold it, after Evelyn had returned to Berlin again.
Later the sale of the car brought Agnese six thousand Euro that she also kept.

Although Evelyn had taken the troubled to take care of everything, she was as well accused by Agnese; that car-keys to have stolen, and as these she later again found, she has not decided necessary herself to apologize.
Elena had called the whole relationship with the accusation that Evelyn wanted to snatch the condominium from Agnese and she wanted then her on the street put down.

Mimmo's ash was not yet buried, as Agnese and Elena by telephone already speculations did over Evelyn death and whoever will be heir to her.

On the seventeenth August, with a taxi Evelyn and Agnese picked up the urn with Mimmo's ash at the crematory of Lambrate and brought it to the graveyard of Baggio. There, it was buried in an urn-compartment near the remains of the brother Angelo.
In the afternoon on the day after it, Evelyn left Milan by train, and arrived in Berlin Spandau on the nineteenth August at half seven o'clock.

Agnese is caught up and ran over from her spiteful past (2007-2009)

Back to Berlin, Evelyn did plans for a definite return to Italy then she knew, that she would live only few years. Therefore, she wanted to die in Italy.

Agnese tried Evelyn to persuade, that she should live with her. As return she should inherit later the apartment.
Agnese believed, that with the apartment she could buy the Evelyn's blessing and therefore she would forgive her because of her spiteful past.

Evelyn made clear to her as a result again to the most umpteen time, that she is not venal, and it was not possible also for many other reasons to pull in the apartment, among other things:
► Even if she would forgive her, she could live together with her on no account then she would perish. ◄
► On health-reasons, she could climb not many stairways. The apartment lay in the second level however and was without elevator. ◄
► That Evelyn suffered from acute depressions, she required her free-space for herself. ◄
► Not too forgotten, if Evelyn inherited the apartment, then she would have had an ongoing war with Elena, even if she had assured her orally, not to want to have the apartment. ◄
Therefore Evelyn wanted to have one-room-apartment for rent that she could pay also herself. But although Agnese and uncles Vittorio allegedly had troubled themselves to find one, no one could be found allegedly.

Agnese had an old- and widow-pension. Lately she had sold the car of Mimmo and with it she would have to have twelve thousand Euro on the bank account. Yet she still had the insolence to claim, that she would have no money.
She knew that Evelyn had only one invalid-pension of less than seven hundred Euro, and nevertheless she tried to beg her.
Did Agnese believe anything, that Evelyn would extra go on the game for her, only because she could not have sufficiently?

After that again Evelyn fell into acute depressions with nervous breakdown. She saw her whole life running out like a film. All memories came back, also that, that she had repressed since eternities, so that she thought beginning of the year 2008 about it, wonder if she should finite write a book about her life.

Evelyn wrote in her digital diary among other things following:
► **Wednesday, the 28 May 2008**
Today, I am exactly 56 years old. Agnese, my wrong mother, has called me at 8:45 o'clock.
- She called me with three different names, but no one of the three was my.
- I gave her to understand, that there were no proof, that she is my mother.
- She denied that and claimed insistent to be.
- I asked her when I was born.
- She said after some seconds thinks: 1952.
- I asked her about the day and the month. Although today I have birthday, she was not capable to answer me!

After 13 minutes telephoning I said, that I don't do well and hung up.
Shortly after the telephone call of Agnese, I began to write the history of my life.
I gave the book the double-title {"Who is Dea APHRODITEKALI?" or "I Fioretti di san Francesco d'Assisi"}, and "Dea APHRODITEKALI" as authoress-name (my artist-name). ◄

► **Thursday, the 19 June 2008**
As I came home back today, I determined that already three times Agnese had tried to call me. That was about 12:30, 12:32 and 12:36 o'clock.
I have called back at 13:16 o'clock.
- She told me, that she was brought to the graveyard in order to visit Angelo and Mimmo.
- I remained cold and gave her to understand, that I had already begun to write my true history, that I would write the truth about everything, above all over my birth and the first eight years of my life. So all and also the relationship will experience the truth, particularly over her.
- She gave herself indifferently and said, that the relationship already know the truth. She accused me to have a nervous breakdown.
- I answer her that the relationship knows only her lies.
- She accuses me to be insane.
- I tell her, that I am with the nerves in the end and I have no time to lose, because I must write the book ready. Therefore, I could call her no longer.

At 13:30 o'clock, I throw down the telephone-earpiece. ◄

► **Tuesday, the 15 July 2008**

Today in the time from 11:21 to 11:29 o'clock, the ex-colleague and friend of Mimmo, Mrs. Luigina called over the telephone in the house of Agnese, because Agnese didn't have the courage to speak directly with me and also in order to have a witness.

- Very kindly, Luigina informed herself about my health.
- After I have told her, that I am with the nerves on the end, I inform her, that I write my true history and also regarding the whole truth over Agnese, that she is no saint, as she believes it everywhere wants to do.
- She tells me, that she is a joy to read my book, when it is written, and she asks me whether I will still to be in contact with Agnese.
- I tell her, that I have it enough to hear the lies from Agnese, concerning my birth and the following years. Until she doesn't tell me the truth, and that she doesn't get for me the medical documentation from my birth and the following eight years, I want to know nothing more of her. Besides, I make the offer for her, that I will give her still time for it at most until I to finishes has written the book. But if I have written it, I can her no longer forgives and will report her.
- Luigina says, that Agnese said, that she loves me.
- I dispute that and say, that I know, that it is not true and that Agnese does everything with calculation.

After we have said goodbye, I finish the telephone call. ◄

► **Sunday, the 27 July 2008**

Today is it exactly one year ago, that Mimmo is dead. I use the opportunity; him, the other relationship and friends, that already dead is, to ask they for advice, through the dice of the future, about Agnese.

- I ask them whether I should still to be in contact with Agnese, if she is the whole truth ready to confess.
- They answer me through the dice, with a very clear ***"no"***, that there is no hope more.
- I ask them whether it is good, that I continue to write my true history, and the truth over Agnese.
- Their answer is a very clear ***"yes"***, because only so the truth about Agnese and me will come to light.

Although the advices from the deceased are beyond all doubt, I have called Agnese exactly at 16:30 o'clock, the moment in that Mimmo died. In the same moment in that she spoke, a very cold shudder ran through my whole body.

I immediately hang up, the deceased are hundred percent in the right, and I know, that it is the last time, that I have called her. ◄

► **Tuesday, the 7 Octobers 2008**
Today I have written to uncles Vittorio. I sent him congratulations to his seventieth-third birthday that is at the 31-10-2008.
At the opportunity I made attentive him on it, that I write a book about my true history, and that I have written also about the event of the August 1959, but I have mention him opposite, what happened in that month.
After all he still had to know exactly, that at that time I was something more than seven years and he was somewhat fewer than twenty-four years old, and we together had had a sexual relations... ◄

► **Friday, the 5 December 2008**
Today I have sent at about fifteen relations the presentation of the book over my "true" lives.
In the next days, I will send it also to other relations, friends and acquaintances from the past.
The presentation I have written like follows:
Christmas 2008 & New Year's Day 2008-2009
Sweetheart relatives, friends, acquaintances and etc etc,
I introduce you officially: The book about my "true" lives and me.
Most of you know me as Evelyn TURIANO, since about ten years in the Internet as "Madame Evelyn TURIANO"...
Others of you knows me already at least as I about seven years old was also as "Dea APHRODITE", since about thirty years and since about ten years also in the Internet as "Dea APHRODITE-KALI"...
By "Dea APHRODITE-KALI" is it about my name of that "varied talents", a so-called artist-name, in this case, my name as "authoress" – "Dea APHRODITE-KALI" writes, in Italian, in German and in English about that "true" history of Evelyn TURIANO... ◄

► **Tuesday, the 16 December 2008**
Today during the weekly cleaning of the apartment, I remembered at it, as I was ten years old:
In year 1962 a limousine halted before the villa in the E.-Vismara-Street 34 (Arese). A nun accompanies from an eminence, one introduced to me as cousin of Agnese. She had come extra from Rome, in order to visit me. I had immediately recognized her as my true mother, the nun, who had left me, after she has born me... ◄

Agnese

06. August 2007

► **Sunday, the 21 December 2008**
Today at 14 o'clock and 43 minutes, me was a dreadful shudder
beyond the back. I became very cold and my body began to tremble very
strongly. The telephone rang in the same moment.
I immediately suspected who the one was: Actually, Agnese had the
freshness to call me despite all:
- She wished me a good Christmas time.
- I asked her why she had called me.
- She announced me, that she had to would be operated at the eyes.
- I asked her, why she refused continuously to confess the truth over
  my birth, and that I remember everything.
- She claimed, that I me deceives, she tried to excite compassion,
  and repeated, that her eyes had to would be operated.
- I asked her with coolness again, why she has called, and that I
  want to know the truth officially.
- She repeated continuously that I me badly deceives and that I
  becomes perish.
- I assured, that she would see it, if my book will be published, and
  finished the telephone call.

The telephone call lasted no longer than four minutes; nevertheless my
body-temperature was cooled down under 35 degrees Celsius.
After about two hours, I was forced to go buys a half kilo of noodles and
cheese, therefore my biological central-heater to take in function
again. ◄

► **Thursday, the 19 February 2009**
Today at 08:16 o'clock has called me my sister Elena. I notice, that
certain falseness is hidden in her voice. She has inherited it certain from
Agnese.
- She announced me that something happened with Agnese.
- I asked her whether Agnese would be dead.
- She answers in the negative and said, that she had been put up in
  an age-home, and that Agnese wanted to die at home.
- I told her about my suspicion concerning my birth, and that Agnese
  extremely probably is not my mother. She is probably a cousin of
  my mother, the one nun was. I told her also some family-secrets.

After some conversation-exchange we finished the telephone call after
about nine minutes. ◄

► **Tuesday, the 24 February 2009**
Today in the time between 11:10 and 11:15 o'clock, on the way back
to home of the usual shopping, my feelings of the soul and the body
changed abruptly and went up and down like a carousel.

I get these feelings, if a person, whom I know, dies or happens
somewhat dreadful to her.
I am immediately sure, that Agnese is dead or lies in dying. In any case, I
hope with whole heart that then is not about somebody other. ◄

► **Wednesday, the 25 February 2009**
It is already since this morning, as I have wakened up and also during
the sleep, that my feelings play carousel up and down.
It is too many and simultaneous information, that I receive from my dear
relatives, friends, acquaintances and advisers from the empire of the
deceased. There is something between them that tries to disturb the
broadcasts. It will probably be Agnese.
Against 11:28 o'clock I tried to call Elena, in orders to experience, who
is deceased, but no one answered. Maybe she is not at home or she
could not come to telephone.
I decide to call in the evening, but then I think, that it is better to wait.
During the evening partly have calmed down me.
The information that I receive from the empire of the deceased is
unambiguous.
They recommend me to protect the calmness, that I am the only person,
who will have uncovered the truth, through my true history and
concerning the experiments in the fifties years and after it.
The book must write and published at all costs, all victims reckon with
me.
It is about twenty-three days that I am terrorized for about twenty-five
times on the day by telephone. Fortunately, I possess the FRITZ!Box®.
So, I can close off the telephone calls with anonymous number. ◄

Since February 2009, as Agnese became conscious, that Evelyn is firm
decided to write the book finished, to publish and to report her after it;
Agnese lost each vitality and decided to die about consequently to
escape a prosecution.
Elena smelled ago chance in orders to inherit everything of Agnese,
although she had not taken care of Agnese since over twenty years.
She knew also, that Evelyn was very sick and she had an acute nervous
breakdown since over one year.
Elena had done only so as if she took care of Agnese. In reality, she
induced Agnese to sign a will only to her favored, and secure to go, she
had an authority given in order to be able to sell the apartment, and so to
secure most for her.
Elena had Agnese put into the age-home although Agnese wanted to die
to house, with the reason, that she herself was too sick in order to take
care of her. As alibi, she went to the cure.

Evelyn could endure her disfigured face no longer. So since about one year, she troubled to have operated itself, on own expenses at the plastic surgeon Dr. Detlef Witzel.
First Dr. Witzel was ready for about ten thousand Euro, operationally, to correct the scars, the face, forehead and neck with a facelift, new to shape the nose, to change the eye-part so like a paradise-bird and to make almond-eyes.
Dr. Witzel has then but for about six months everything only excess hesitated; because he, instigated from his colleagues Dr. Olaf Kauder and Mrs. Dr. Cara Tjaden-Müller in Berlin-Spandau, he trusted no longer to operate.
Despite strong misgivings, Evelyn didn't remain other as to go to the Dr. Dr. med. Johannes C. Bruck in the Martin-Luther-Hospital in Berlin-Schmargendorf.
Dr. Bruck operated Evelyn on the twenty-sixth May 2009 in the hospital „Clinica Vita" in Berlin-Wilmersdorf, for the proud amount of about fifteen thousand Euro. First, the face looked beautiful and young, because it was swollen, but little by little Evelyn determined, that made completely sloppy, and also the extra-wishes were not done.
Dr. Bruck tried to persuade Evelyn, that everything was in order and refused her renewed and perfectly to operate, so that in November Evelyn was forced to engage the Laux-lawyers to represent her interests.

Since Evelyn had started to write the book, in her living seemed like to be bewitched.
It was not enough, that again she had depressions and a nervous breakdown.
No, as well some doctors-practices had to been against her, e. g. the medical personnel of the gynecologist-practice from Mrs. Dr. Sorina Kunert & colleagues, that later they were moved to the number four the Haberland-Way in Berlin-Staaken.
They tried Evelyn to convince, that supposedly because of a new law she had to would pay her the essential and most necessary hormone-preparation, although that the health insurance company had denied it.
On the twenty-first April 2009, Evelyn made clear that she knows exactly her right.
As countermove, she was offended heavily from the medical personnel and she was bombarded downright with racists (foreigners-hostiles), handicapped-people-hostiles and misanthropies, disdainful expressions.
Two days later, Evelyn had written a complaint-letter per certified-letter with return-certificate personally at Mrs. Dr. Sorina Kunert to sent. The letter was not only ignored, but as countermove Evelyn received a

telephone call of the doctor-helper with the communication, that the gynecologist-practice wanted no longer to treat her.

Mrs. Dr. Cara Tjaden-Müller prescribed Evelyn an antibiotic-containing medication for months, although she knew, that Evelyn is allergic with it. Then she sabotaged Evelyn's plans for the face-operation.

Dr. Witzel, instigated through his colleagues Dr. Olaf Kauder and Mrs. Dr. Cara Tjaden-Müller, he wanted now no longer to operate Evelyn.

Dr. Bruck had failed the face-operation and he refused she renews and perfectly to operate.

The senior consultant professor Dr. med. D. Elling in the "Sana-Clinical-Complex" in Berlin-Lichtenberg, who had enforced a vaginal-correction by Evelyn at September 2009, he had not operated like arranged, so that the same problems had remained after it.

Evelyn brought him to account, but he denied everything.

It is always advisable to bring at least one witnesses, if one going to the senior consultant professor Dr. med. D. Elling consulting hours.

Remarkably there were also constantly problems with the personnel-computer. It looked so, as if somebody from outside tried, continues to penetrate in order to enforce sabotage. But Evelyn had made provisions and she had memorized several copies of the book in different media memory.

At the beginning of June 2009, at few days after Evelyn face-operations, Evelyn received from Elena of a SMS with the request about call back. Elena declared during the telephones call, that according to statements of the doctors Agnese had only to live a few weeks.

Evelyn explained that she is newly operated, and that therefore she doesn't can to Italy comes, even if she wanted - because of the height of the infection-danger.

Oddly enough the telephone-terror had stopped since some days. The depressions and the nervous breakdown were almost like in air dissolved and Evelyn was unequivocally calmer.

On the twenty-second June 2009 at seven o'clock and forty-five minutes, Evelyn's worst enemy Agnese was dead, in an age-home in Casalnoceto province of Alessandria, Italy.

Shortly after eight o'clock Evelyn received a SMS from Elena with the sentence: "The mommy is dead".

Evelyn had pronounced to the relationship the condolence by telephone, but Elena and aunt Silvana had rejected each time the telephone call on purpose.

Elena got to do Agnese buries in the mausoleum of the families Dossola, although Agnese wanted to become bury expressly and testamentary in Baggio.

Giovanni, the deceased husband of Elena and the remaining dead of the family Dossola would turn in their grave if they knew, that Agnese was buried in the same mausoleum.
With the time one will determine, that it haunts in the Dossola mausoleum, since also Agnese lies there.

Since over thirty years, Evelyn had put an eternally curse over Agnese's soul. She should be born as hermaphrodite again and again, and she experiences all ailments, that Evelyn had to endure in the first eight years of her life.
Only Dea APHRODITE-KALI has the power to cancel this curse again, and no one of the others gods can stand by Agnese's soul or her protect. This curse is only annulling, if Agnese's soul becomes consciously about the damage, that she has caused at Evelyn and also she regrets it.

Whoever quarrels with Dea APHRODITE-KALI, must not be surprised, if whoever to pull itself the anger from the Gods!

Hermaphrodite-creatures have the gift to bless, but even the power to curse!

The start of a new era (?) (2009-2011)

Elena tried as quickly as possibly to sell Agnese's apartment, and to dissolve Agnese's bank account, but without Evelyn's consent, that was impossible for her.
Monday, that twenty-ninth June 2009, Evelyn received a telephone call of a certain geometer Mr. Arrigone Gian Piero from Castellar Guidobono (Alessandria), in the order and presence of Elena.
The geometer told, that Agnese's will was opened and that only Elena is heiress.
Evelyn made clear to him, that in any case she has a right on the legal portion.
He said on the other hand, that it would be no problem, because Elena wants to divide. With it however he wanted to persuade Evelyn, that the apartment would not be much value on the basis of the economy-crisis. Evelyn made clear to him on the other hand, that she would not be stupid and that she exactly know, that that apartment has a value from about hundred-sixty thousand Euro, because some months before it a neighbor had sold an exactly same apartment for about two hundred-thousand Euro.

On the fourth July, completely hidden from Evelyn, secretly Elena had deposit and publishes Agnese's holographic will at the notary Dr. Vincenso Esposito in Tortona (Alessandria).
Agnese had written the will certain under influence from Elena.
Agnese always had a writing like a hen, but this will, that been written on half ruled notebook-leaf, seemed as would have been written it by a hen that under drugs was put down.

Quotation of the will:
▶ "Will
I revoke each of my preceding wills.
I nominate to the universal-heir of all, which I will possess in the moment of my death, my daughter Turiano Elena.
I wish to be buried on the graveyard of the community of Baggio.
Casalnoceto, 25-04-2009,
Fioraso Agnese" ◀

In a telephone conversation with Elena on the same day, as she had deposited and published the will, Evelyn noticed that Elena didn't want to divide the inheritance. The opposite was the case.

Elena warped all words that Evelyn said and she claimed, that Evelyn would have refused in writing the inheritance, what was not the case. Evelyn made Elena unequivocally clear, that she would not have refused at all, that she didn't intend to waive her right and if it became necessary, then she would sue lawfully her right.

On the sixth July, through e-mail Evelyn engaged the lawyer Mrs. Attilia Fracchia to represent her interests, that meanwhile she had moved to the number eight at the Kaiser-Tito-Place in Milan.
After inquiry of the situation, the lawyer took on the case.

Elena immediately received panic as she experienced that a lawyer represents Evelyn.
For a short time, she was even ready to give up the inheritance to favor of Evelyn, although she had made a few days before unequivocally clear, that she and her family wanted nothing knows from Evelyn. But Evelyn insisted on just division between the sisters.

In the following months, the woman-lawyer was really sabotaged and held out from Elena and her "specialist" geometers Arrigone Gian Piero, for example they refused to hand over that statement of account of the last two years of Agnese's bank account.

On the twenty-first September, shortly before seventeen o'clock, Elena tried to play the compassion-tour during a telephonic conversation with Evelyn, but Evelyn didn't fall for it and made clear to her, if she doesn't collaborate with the woman-lawyer, then nothing other remains as to take legal proceedings.
Elena tried it further with the compassion-tour. It came to the dispute. Evelyn said that she should be ashamed and that she itself just as maliciously as Agnese would have behaved, and after it she hung up.

On the next day, Elena played the same compassion-tour with the woman-lawyer of Evelyn by telephone.
The woman-lawyer made clear Elena that Evelyn wants to do no war against her, but if she didn't collaborate, then nothing other remains, than to take legal proceedings. So, Elena remained nothing other as to yield.

After Evelyn at the Italian consulate in Berlin, from notary has prepared a document, that the woman-lawyer made to her special-representative; on the twenty-fourth November Elena had to do legitimizes at the notary Dr. Vincenso Esposito, that Evelyn is entitled to one third of the inheritance.

Since November, with notary was officially certificated, that Evelyn is joint heir of one third, nevertheless Elena and her "specialist" the geometer tried still to prevent the dissolution and division of the inheritance.

End of January, Evelyn's woman-lawyer received from the bank that from her ordered statement of account, from the last two years of the deceased.
The documentations from the statement of account had resulted, that the last two months up to the death of Agnese, from her account one embezzled through several bank-checks a total of about seventeen-thousand Euro, although already since over two months Agnese in dying lay.

Evelyn, that suspected exactly, who the embezzlement had committed, induced as a result, that the woman-lawyer engaged the bank to enforce an exact examination.
As soon as the confirmation was available, that Elena had to be responsible for the embezzlement, she should be pursued criminally and for it is worried, that she loses her right as heiress.
In March, Evelyn reported the uncles Pierino (Pietro), Vittorio and the aunt Silvana of Elena's embezzlement.
Furthermore, in order certainly to go, that Elena receives the just penalty, Evelyn in writing cursed her, her descendants and all her accomplices.

The out of court lawsuit against Dr. Dr. med. Johannes C. Bruck, because of the total slipshod face-operation, had no End in view.
[…] ⇔ [Dr. Dr. med. Johannes C. Bruck has reached, that stood word-sentence into this position, through temporary injunction (decision of Country-Court Berlin of the 26. August 2010, records-number: 27 O 662/10) from Evelyn had must to remove. – This judgment would be decided in absence and without knowledge of Evelyn. – In the contradiction-process and appeal-process Evelyn had the strong impression (at least is of the personal opinion of Evelyn (Articles 5 of the German constitution)), that the court and consequently "the senate" no interests had the facts to go on the reason. – Well yes, by different social class becomes of course a with multiple "doctor-titles" more believed as somebody of low class like Evelyn, that is Evelyn's personal opinion! (Articles 5 of the German constitution)* – The question is also, whether a court decision, that "only" from a judicial employee is signed, actually final is?]*

(Articles 5 of the German constitution) (1) Everyone has the right, her/his opinion in word, writing and picture freely to express and to spread, and itself from generally accessible sources unhindered to inform. The freedom of the presses and the freedom of the reporting through broadcasting and, is films guaranteed. A censorship doesn't take place.*

Dr. Dr. med. Johannes C. Bruck had also, in order to get out of the affair, a liquidation-bill with absurd performances submitted, as well as: ten times transplantation a sinew or a muscle, four times transplants, eleven times nerves-shift and new-embed, four times implantations, two times distance of foreign body and so on.

Dr. Dr. med. Johannes C. Bruck even had not from recoiled Evelyn the diagnosis "Cutis Laxa" to poem, a rare genetic illness of the conjunctiva-tissue. It shall only one hundred and fifty-nine so sicken on the whole world.

The first two items of this liquidation-bill would be put also in bill, that be concerned the date 07 July 2008, although at this day Evelyn was referred to Dr. Dr. med. Johannes C. Bruck with "referral-certificate" because of scar-corrections. Consequently Dr. Dr. med. Johannes C. Bruck had the day 07 July 2008 doubly collects, once from that health insurance company (that AOK) and from Evelyn.

As Evelyn's woman-lawyer in writing put Dr. Dr. med. Johannes C. Bruck to speak, answer his lawyers with date of the 07 May 2010 next quotations: << The indication of it at the 07.07.2008 submitted referral-certificate goes in the void, because the patient came also to this time as private-patient to our client. At no time, on the part of the patient was striven an expenses-takeover of the health insurance company. Logically, our client has given the referral-certificate also immediately again back to the patient. >>

In this liquidation-bill would become cashed up, even once under item 10 and once under item 23 anesthesia-performances, although Evelyn had already settled after separated bill putting up of the anesthesia-doctors. – It must also be said, that according to bill of the anesthesia-doctors, the anesthesia-total-time has lasted "only" 165 minutes, although with date of the 07 May 2010, Dr. Dr. med. Johannes C. Bruck's lawyers have claim following quotation: << … On the basis of the considerable duration of the entire operation of well 4 hours was … >>

Under item 29 became calculated moreover tree times detailed written diagnoses, although by the submitted documents was to be taken "only" the operation-report, that remaining an untrue operation-datum contains and according to opinion of Evelyn (Articles 5 of the German constitution)* also not formal it was written.

The statement from Dr. Dr. med. Johannes C. Bruck's lawyers was in the same letter, quotation: << ... 3 detailed written diagnoses were actually executed. In this connection, it is about the operation-report, the treatment-report wished by patient as well as about an writing notification of illness, ... >> – at all Evelyn had demand no one treatment-report and writing notification of illness, and already not at all she has gotten, and to what she should need a writing notification of illness, she has become pension since over 25 years on health-reasons.

The operation of the 26 May 2009, taken place through Dr. Dr. med. Johannes C. Bruck, come like a contractual default. The operation-goal was missed completely, so that the service of Dr. Dr. med. Johannes C. Bruck therefore in the result completely useless and worthless is.
Besides come, that Evelyn was not informed in the advisable manner about risks, especially over success- as well as failure-risks.
On these reasons, on the first April 2010, the Laux-lawyers demanded from Dr. Dr. med. Johannes C. Bruck to acknowledge his compensation-duty and the achieved honorarium plus the expenses for anesthesia, as well as the expenses for the stationary stay to reimburse; on the basis of the § 12 paragraphs 3 GOÄ (settlement and bill of the reimbursement for professional performances of the doctors) and § 280 BGB (compensation because of duty-injuring).
Furthermore Evelyn is to be indemnifying for the pains suffered through the abortive operation and psychic burdens.
Evelyn is ready in any case also through legal proceedings to demand her right.

At the 21 June 2010, the Country-Court Berlin confirmed the receipt (records-number: 35 O 201/10) of the suit against the Doc. Dr. Dr. med. habil. Johannes C. Bruck.

Also with the legal proceedings, the statements of Dr. Dr. med. Johannes C. Bruck as well as his lawyers were last contradictory.
Even had his lawyers, with one letter to the Country-Court Berlin of the 02 September 2010, refer on, quotation: << ... 2. Hearing of the defendant according to §§ 444, 448 ZPO ... >>
§§ 444 ZPO meant: << **Consequences the elimination of a document**: A document is from a party in the intent, its use the opponent to evade, remove or to the use unsuitable done, so according to the claims of that opponents over the composition and the content of that document can be regarded as proved. >>
Evelyn is of the opinion (Articles 5 of the German constitution)*, if somebody itself appoints on one such paragraph, then such a person is completely implausible.

The Country-Court Berlin had ordered the patient file, medical file, diagnosis-reports, and so on from doctors, hospitals and medical facilities. – So, before court lay too the proof, that really at the 07 July 2008 Evelyn would be refers to Dr. Dr. med. Johannes C. Bruck with "referral-certificate", because of the scar-corrections. With regard to, with date 20 December 2010, Dr. Dr. med. Johannes C. Bruck's lawyer admitted, quotation: << ... 2. At the representation of the plaintiff to content and scope the risk-enlightenment is merely right, that at the 07.07.2008 really she was on the referral-certificate the house-doctor to in the consulting hours of the defendant. ... >>
According to opinion of Evelyn (Articles 5 of the German constitution)*, Dr. Dr. med. Johannes C. Bruck had admitted with it, that he had doubly collected the day of 07.07.2008, once from that health insurance company (that AOK) and from Evelyn, consequently he had made commit an offence of the deceit. – That is of the personal opinion of Evelyn (Articles 5 of the German constitution)*.

On the second May 2011, at the police-precinct in Berlin-Spandau, Evelyn reported Dr. Dr. med. Johannes C. Bruck because of deceit (bill-deceit), (file-number: 110502-1030-025272).

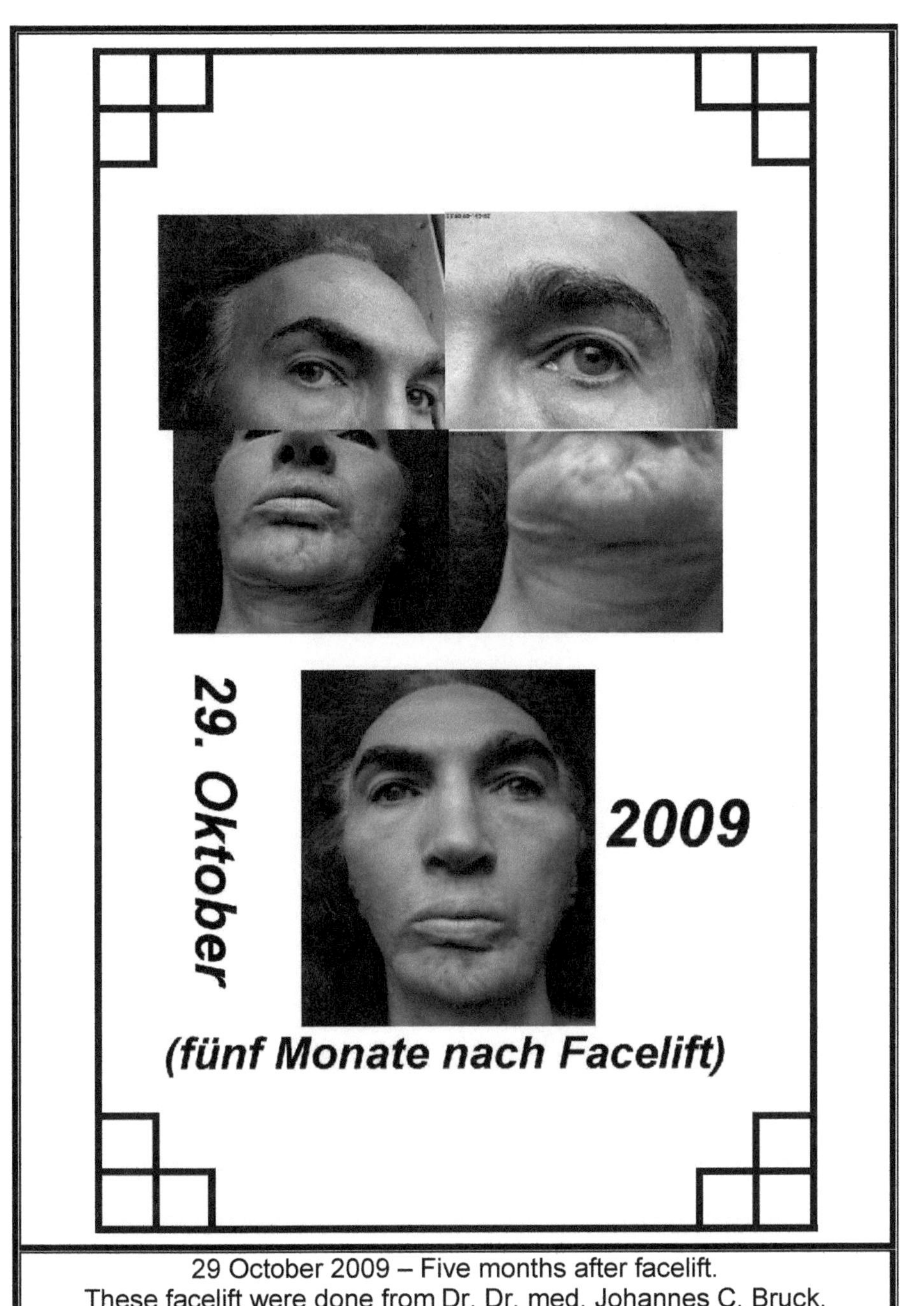

29 October 2009 – Five months after facelift.
These facelift were done from Dr. Dr. med. Johannes C. Bruck.

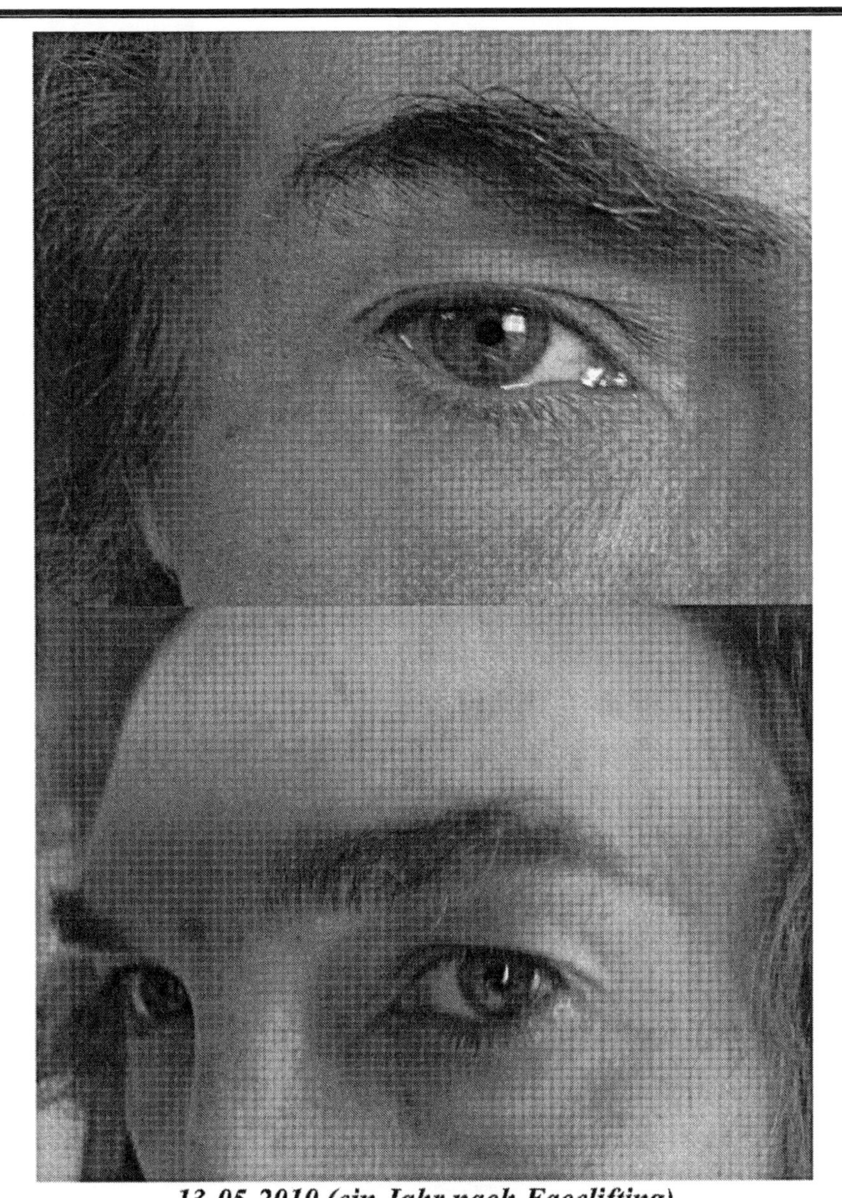

13-05-2010 (ein Jahr nach Facelifting)

13 May 2010 – One year after facelift.
These facelift were done from Dr. Dr. med. Johannes C. Bruck.

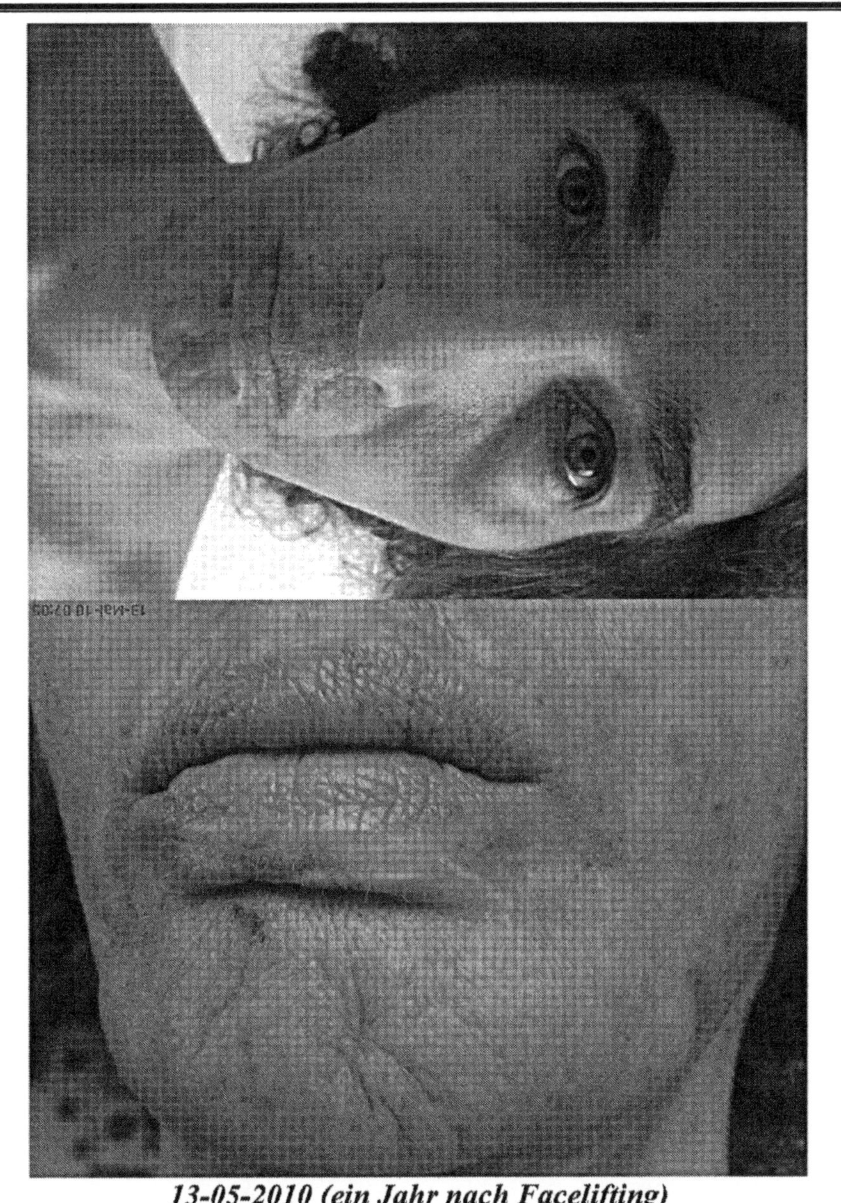

13-05-2010 (ein Jahr nach Facelifting)

13 May 2010 – One year after facelift.
These facelift were done from Dr. Dr. med. Johannes C. Bruck.

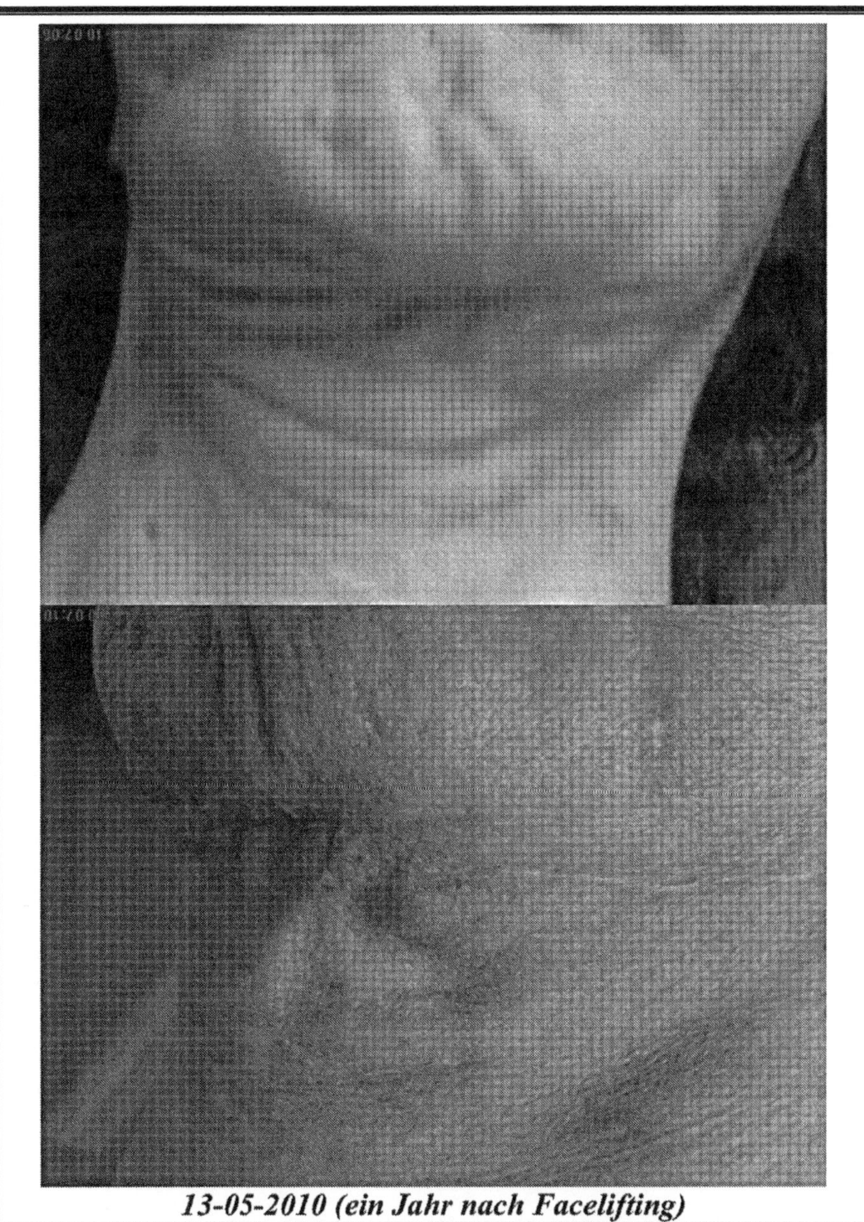

13-05-2010 (ein Jahr nach Facelifting)

13 May 2010 – One year after facelift.
These facelift were done from Dr. Dr. med. Johannes C. Bruck.

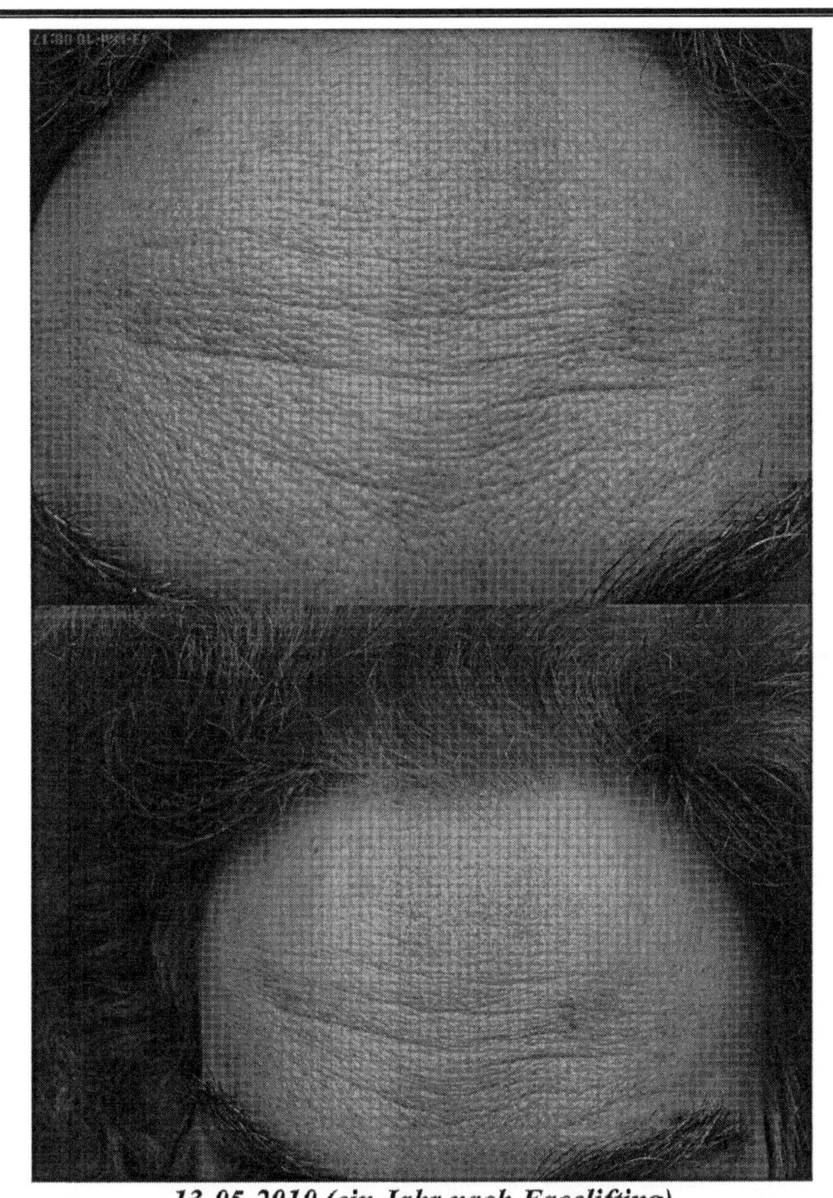

13-05-2010 (ein Jahr nach Facelifting)

13 May 2010 – One year after facelift.
These facelift were done from Dr. Dr. med. Johannes C. Bruck.

Arabic (desire-) dream (-man) (?) (June-July 2011)

Since about a half year, in Evelyn's head haunts the famous last sentence from the more antique Roman Imperator Julius Cesar: ***"You Pluto too!"*** – Julius Cesar has pronounced this sentence, at that time as the then members from the Roman senate murdered him. – Between the murderers was too Julius Cesar's stepson Pluto.
Is this spook an indication of Evelyn's future murderer? – Or is an indication of a future event of Evelyn?

Since years, Evelyn suffers over the noise disturbance and that last cigarette-stubs on her balcony that somebody causes that somewhere over her lives.
As but at the eighteenth June against nine o'clock, she has got up, and she had ascertained, that from the apartment over her one water damage must have taken place, and that her balcony looked how a stubs sanitary landfill, the barrel had gone over.
The goddess Kali got have the upper hand of and went a floor high, she rang stormily to Ali Barakji, as nobody opened, stormily she knock at the door and threatened with the police, in the case that nobody opens.
After short time, a completely sleepy about twenty-second years young Arab opened the door, he was dressed only with trunks. He looked so like a prince from "thousand and a night".
As Evelyn saw he, she had to would strong keep back itself in order to give not the goddess Aphrodite the upper hand.
Without to ask him, stormily Evelyn entered the apartment, in order to see after the right, but it was all dries, therefore must had to be about a damage from the bathtub-outflow.
Nevertheless, Evelyn swung Ali to go down to her apartment, in order to appraise the water damage and the stubs sanitary landfill.
It appearance as Ali was very strongly impressed from the ardently vivacious goddess Kali.

Something a week later, the goddess Dea Aphrodite-Kali wanted to do one more comfortably relay evening, therefore she created herself the appropriate ambience with candles, perfumes and so on.
The room was filled with roses, jasmine, lavenders and other seductive perfumes, as Dea had fallen asleep deeply.
The tomcat Tiger, the assistant of Dea, by plays he went at the candles too near, so that he became fires, at itself and Dea to save, he changes to a fire-bird And he fly across the balcony-door a floor high, where Ali lives.

*As Ali that sees, becomes him consciously that Dea must be in danger,
he immediately runs down to Dea, and because nobody opened, he
smashed with woolen strength the door.*
*Dea lay lifelessly on her heaven-bed; Ali immediately undertook the
rescue-measure in order to rescue Dea.*
*As Dea came to the senses again, fell in love together, and as Dea and
Ali hovered over all clouds, rang at the door.*
Evelyn would become awake, and the dream burst like a bubble. …

… The reality looks differently, as Ali went to Evelyn, the two discussed
over the water-damage and over others.
Evelyn and Ali came themselves mentally near and it had develop one
sibling-like friendship.
Unfortunately not only Evelyn had her problems, but also Ali, so that their
problems always between them will be.
Interesting is too, that Ali internet-user-name is almost hundred percent
the same as **"Pluto"**.

End with predict

It looked so, as if the printing and consequently the publication the history of Evelyn born "FROLETTI" (alias Dea APHRODITE-KALI), intentional one would prevent, although middle of the year 2010 as good as everything ready was written.
Perino Heydemann, a good friend of Evelyn, and first proof-reader (?!?!?) the German version of the manuscript, seem he didn't to want to correct further. Fact is, that for which reason also always, the correction moved on the length.
It also looked so, as if the publishing houses, those Evelyn had sent part-manuscripts, no interest in her history showed, that she first received no answers. The publishing houses, that showed interest, had impossible contract-conditions. According to statements of the model-contract (some so-called subsidized publishers), the author should pay the publication-expenses, the full risk carries, and the lawful copyrights lose and as thanks else as good as only the expenses kept.
Of course, such conditions don't come for Evelyn in asks. She is maybe naive, but not stupid.
However, someday the printing and the publication of the book take his course.

The time will show, whether the death of Agnese, Evelyn's worst enemy, the start of a new era for Evelyn is or not.
Some time after the publication of the book, Evelyn will die on mysterious way. The forensic medicine institute will determine, that she was murdered.
Does the Vatican have to do something with the mysterious death of Evelyn?
At the latest after the mysterious death of Evelyn, the book wills to a bestseller.

1990
Mischita

2001
Kikki Blue

2005
Tiger

Short about Dea APHRODITE-KALI:

- **At the 28 May 1952**, at 13:40 o'clock, in a special-department of a Milanese clinic, in the house No. 52 the Macedonio-Melloni-Street in Milan/Italy (Presidio Ospedaliero Macedonio Melloni - Azienda Ospedaliera Fatebenefratelli e Oftalmico) is a child been born, whose mother not wants recognized. This child turned into Dea APHRODITE-KALI, under others also an authoress of her proper autobiography.
- **Until 1969:** She was getting rid of in different orphanages, nuns convent, children's home and boarding school.
- **November 1969:** She is escape to West Berlin Germany, and in Berlin remained.
- **2008-2010:** She had written her autobiography.
- **<u>She has published:</u>**
    1. **July 20010:** She has published her autobiography in Italian language with the title "Chi è Dea APHRODITE-KALI?" oppure "I Fioretti di san Francesco d'Assisi";
    ISBN 9783839198636, Paperback, 136 pages;
    Books on Demand (publishing house).
    2. **August 2010:** She has published her autobiography in German language with the title "Wer ist Dea APHRODITE-KALI?" oder "I Fioretti di san Francesco d'Assisi";
    ISBN 9783839198612, Paperback, 144 pages;
    Books on Demand (publishing house).
    3. **February 2011:** She has published the second edition her autobiography in Italian language with the title "Chi è Dea APHRODITE-KALI?" oppure "I Fioretti di san Francesco d'Assisi"; ISBN 9783839198636, Paperback, 136 pages; Books on Demand (publishing house).
    4. **24 February 2011:** She has published the "Kindle e-Book" her autobiography in Italian language with the title "Chi è Dea APHRODITE-KALI?" oppure "I Fioretti di san Francesco d'Assisi"; ISBN 9783842314528, 138 pages;
    Books on Demand (publishing house).
    5. **March 2011:** She has published the second edition her autobiography in German language with the title "Wer ist Dea APHRODITE-KALI?" oder "I Fioretti di san Francesco

d'Assisi"; ISBN 9783839198612, Paperback, 144 pages;
Books on Demand (publishing house).

6. **21 March 2011:** She has published the "Kindle e-Book"
   her autobiography in German language with the title "Wer ist
   Dea APHRODITE-KALI?" oder "I Fioretti di san Francesco
   d'Assisi"; ISBN 9783842393134; 146 pages;
   Books on Demand (publishing house).

7. **August 2011:** She has published her autobiography in
   English language with the title "Who is Dea APHRODITE-
   KALI?" or "I Fioretti di san Francesco d'Assisi";
   ISBN 9783842375260, Paperback, 156 pages;
   Books on Demand (publishing house).

8. **August 2011:** She has published the "Kindle e-Book" her
   autobiography in English language with the title "Who is Dea
   APHRODITE-KALI?" or "I Fioretti di san Francesco d'Assisi";
   ISBN (Yet not known)
   Books on Demand (publishing house).

Imprint

The German national-library records this publication in the German national-bibliography; elaborate bibliographical data are accessible in the Internet under http://dnb.d-nb.de

Editor:

Evelyn TURIANO
Postfach 200355
D-13513 Berlin
Germany

© 2010, 2011 Copyright by Evelyn TURIANO & Dea APHRODITE-KALI
Berlin - Germany
All right reservations.

Authoress and translator to English language:

Dea APHRODITE-KALI
Postfach 200355
D-13513 Berlin
Germany

{The authoress and editor refers on theirs right at the "articles 5 that German Constitution"!}

1. Edition August 2011

Production and publishing house:

Books on Demand GmbH, Norderstedt, Germany

ISBN 9783842375260